A POSITION OF TRUST

By the same author

The Gadfly Summer

A POSITION OF TRUST

ROY HART

St. Martin's Press
New York

For Tricia and Christopher,
Gina and John and Stewart

A POSITION OF TRUST. Copyright © 1985 by Roy Hart. All rights reserved. Printed in the United States of America. No part of this book may be used or reproduced in any manner whatsoever without written permission except in the case of brief quotations embodied in critical articles or reviews. For information, address St. Martin's Press, 175 Fifth Avenue, New York, N.Y. 10010.

Library of Congress Cataloging in Publication Data

Hart, Roy.
    A position of trust.

    I. Title.
PR6058.A694857P6   1985   823'.914   85-12524
ISBN 0-312-63186-3

First published in Great Britain by Robert Hale Ltd.
First U.S. Edition
10 9 8 7 6 5 4 3 2 1

A POSITION OF TRUST

One

From the bridge in St. James's Park, early on a misty summer morning, the view towards Whitehall may occasionally be seen in apotheosis; no longer the dour rooftops of government, but another kingdom at far remove, an enchanted place of softly outlined gables and spires and minarets beyond a hazy screen of distant trees.

At seven o'clock that June morning, however, neither of the two men crossing the bridge was in the mood for romantic imagery. Darkly suited and briefcased, each was clearly an archetypal courtier in the kingdom beyond the trees.

At the middle of the bridge, the taller of the two men broke stride, and then stopped and hooked his umbrella over the rail, and then took from his briefcase a brown paper bag. The other man turned in beside him.

'A drip, Tony?' the taller man enquired. 'Or a leak is it?'

'A bloody great leak,' replied the other. 'Mingay had me out of bed at four o'clock this morning to tell me so.' With his umbrella hanging from his wrist he was taking his cigarette-case from his waistcoat.

The taller man, Tribe, had opened the paper bag; and that the ducks were his familiars was already evidenced by the vee-shaped wakes that were centreing upon him. At this time of the morning he much preferred ducks to people. He cast out a handful of neatly diced bread cubes.

The other man, Quilter, flipped open his cigarette-case and held it out over the rail where his companion could see it.

'According to Mingay,' he said. 'It might go back ten years.'

Tribe glanced down at the case. 'No, thank you, Tony,' he said. 'How do we know exactly? What little bird's blown the gaff?' A cube of bread, balanced on a hooked forefinger, was flicked away with a thumbnail in the direction of a particularly handsome mallard.

'The stuff of dreams, David,' replied Quilter, around the cigarette he was trying to light against a momentary breeze. 'Or perhaps nightmare would be a better word. Someone at Moscow Centre. A potential defector wooing Washington. Making a display of his possible wares; offering proof of goodwill as it were.' He snapped his lighter shut and slipped it back into his waistcoat.

'And credible?'

'Oh, yes. Indeed he is.'

Another cube of bread was aimed for the favoured mallard.

'A filing clerk?'

'A ranking General – according to Washington. Second Directorate.'

Tribe stretched his mouth reflectively. He had reached an age where little surprised him.

'And what does the General want?'

'The same as all the others,' said Quilter. 'Resettlement. A quiet retirement; and the usual remuneration, of course.'

Tribe upended the empty paper bag and shook the last few crumbs out over the water.

'And what's he presently putting out?'

'Presently us,' replied Quilter. 'My Section in the particular. One of my staff has been feeding this man; and he in his turn has fed a few samples back to Washington. Authentic. All Grade-A goods.'

The paper bag was folded, and pressed flat on the rail with a couple of sweeping gestures, then returned to the briefcase for use again tomorrow. Tribe walked on across the bridge and Quilter fell into step again beside him.

'Is this man of yours prepared to name names yet?'

'Not until he comes over,' replied Quilter. 'I don't blame him; it's one of the ground-rules.'

'And when does he propose to join us?'

'We don't know.' Quilter dropped his cigarette-end at the end of the bridge and trod it out. 'Washington wants him to stay in place until the current trade-talks finish in Geneva. A defection just now could be an embarrassment. To both sides.'

They passed the bandstand and stepped on to Horse Guard's Parade. Around its perimeter gangs of workmen were setting up scaffolding for Saturday's Trooping of the Colour.

Tribe made a stab at the parade ground with the ferrule of his umbrella like a park-keeper spiking up litter.

'It could be another Centre ploy,' he suggested. 'Have you thought about that? Someone in Dzerzhinski Square getting us all sniffing up each other's backsides. Teasing us all to rip each other's throats out. Sverdlov. His métier that was. He broke our bloody hearts and poor old George Foster had to resign. Remember?'

'History, David,' countered Quilter. And a slice of it that Clive Mingay did not wish to see repeated. That was something else that he had seen fit to mention at four o'clock this morning.

Tribe walked on with his gaze downward. He was, thank God, close to retirement. When he had first entered this grubby business, he had believed that treachery had a certain smell, something akin to the odour of old running shoes; or a craftily dropped shoulder or a shifty look. That philosophy was long gone. An efficient traitor was a personable man; for some reason women were not attracted to treachery on the grand scale. Most women spied for the love of a man. Men spied for themselves, for vanity, for spite; or for the cause, whatever that was. They were dreamers, pie in the sky men, or axe grinders, and sometimes, but not often, devoted workers for the cause of a corporate social order that they had never experienced at first hand. Few who had ever seen the system that close ever chose to work for it.

'I'll want the dossiers of all your old lags,' he said, of a sudden. 'Anybody who goes back ten years or more.'

'I've got eight of them like that,' said Quilter. 'So you've got your work cut out. And Mingay wants a quick result. Preferably yesterday.'

'I'm not going off at half-cock,' snapped Tribe irritably. 'And what I'm not is a bloody magician.'

They walked into the shadow of the guardhouse archway and came out into the sunlight again between the Treasury and the old Admiralty building. The rush-hour was yet to come and Whitehall was eerily quiet. They crossed it to the shaded pavement of the other side.

'What about ideas of your own, Tony? Got any?'

'No,' said Quilter. 'I wish I had.'

They stopped on the corner of Horse Guards Avenue.

'But you'll work on it?'

'Assiduously,' replied Quilter.

They shook hands, then Tribe turned to march northwards up Whitehall, his umbrella sloped across his shoulder like a sabre; but only for five or six paces before he stopped and turned back again.

'Don't discount anybody, will you, Tony. Not even your most tried and trusted. – And when we find the bugger we'll nail him to the wall together. Good-day to you.'

Quilter trod up the steps to his office, and Tribe resumed his brisk march towards Trafalgar Square.

Two

Coast crossed Whitehall in the bright morning sunshine, stopping once on an island to let a bus go by in the direction of Westminster, then breaking into a clumsy lumbering trot to reach the other side. He took the four steps up from the pavement in two brisk strides and pushed through the brass-handled swing doors into the fussily Edwardian entrance hall.

The display of his pass was only a formality. The elderly security guard saluted him. 'Morning, Mr. Coast. Nice to see you, sir. Good trip?'

'Yes, Sam. Very pleasant. Daughter's wedding go off all right, did it?'

"Yes, sir, just fine. She's in Majorca now, sunning herself.'

'Not alone, I hope?'

The guard chuckled hugely after Coast's departing back. Of all the gentlemen who worked on the fourth floor Mr. Coast was the only one who always stopped for a word and sometimes a joke – and took the trouble to remember what his name was.

He smoked a cigarette while he cast an eye over the papers that had accumulated in his trays while he had been in Paris. They were mostly trivial; this was the dead season. A few inter-Section memos, some low-graded signals that Quilter had sent in out of courtesy to keep him up to date, a note from the treasurer of the squash-club reminding that his half-yearly subscription was imminently due. Not that he had played for years, but it was important to belong; just as it was important to have been to the right schools and to wear the right ties, and not be seen to be in debt or homosexual.

Then he went to the filing-cabinet beside the door, unlocking it and dragging open each of the drawers in turn. His markers, small flags of paper sticking up innocently like bookmarks here and there, were exactly as he had left them.

By nine-fifteen his jacket was off and he was drafting a résumé of the meeting with Peterson for Quilter. It had been like bargaining with a raddled old harlot who was coyly pretending virginity. He heard Wesley unlocking his office next door, then Cyril Toler further along the passage; then the purr of the coffee-machine accompanied by the harsh dry cough of the chronic bronchitic, both of which heralded the invariably later arrival of Eric Lomax.

At ten he dashed his sprawling signature beneath the last paragraph and buzzed through to Wesley, who came through the connecting door buttoning his jacket.

Rooted at Cambridge and re-potted at Camberley, certain of young Wesley's gestures were still faintly martial, and only just did he not stamp his feet together as he stopped on the far side of the desk.

'I didn't know you were back, Mr. Coast. I'm sorry.'

'That's all right, Roger. I caught the evening flight yesterday.' He slid forward the wooden casket he kept on his desk for visitors. 'Take a seat, old chap. Have a cigarette.'

Wesley was yet another of the unhewn boys who thought that polishing their trouser-seats all day in this particular branch of the Firm would eventually place them among a glamorous elect. It rarely happened. Most fell by the wayside out of boredom, and the rest were harassed into resignation by doting young wives who saw in their husband's reluctance to discuss their work the incipient manifestations of marital disloyalty.

'Any alarms or excursions?'

'Very quiet, sir.' Lomax had been on leave last Thursday. There had been a brief flurry of telexes from Ankara on Friday morning; those telexes now so much fish and chip paper.

Little things, but important. When Coast was away, Wesley was his eyes and ears and passer on of washroom tittle-tattle; and very often one little snippet of gossip could be jigsawed into another and become significant.

'And on Friday evening, the security people stopped Goldie on her way out and searched her handbag. They found a key in it – not on a ring. It was a new one she had had cut for her flat. I think she had some difficulty proving it – she hadn't picked up the bill or something.

'But nothing to shake the Universe, eh?'

Wesley's smile was much like Coast's. Quickly contrived and switched off in a moment. He wouldn't go far, he was too obviously a watcher.

'No, sir,' he said, and seemed disappointed that he had not been more efficient. 'Except,' he added, with a diffidence unusual in him. 'I'm getting married, sir. Audrey Spencer.'

Miss Spencer ran the small typing-pool downstairs. A tall, thin young woman who leaned sharply forward when she walked, her most noteworthy attraction lay in the several hundred acres owned by her father a few miles out of Chelmsford, in Essex.

'That's splendid news. My very good wishes to both of you.'

'We've arranged it for July. The first Saturday. Audrey and I – well – we'd like you to come.'

'Of course. I'd be delighted. Thank you.'

It took a moment for Wesley to realise that he had been dismissed. He rose, and swung his chair back into place exactly as it had been, then stubbed out his cigarette.

Coast passed him the résumé.

'For Goldie, Roger. I'd like it back before eleven – and an appointment with Mr. Q. before lunch. Arrange that, will you?'

'Will do, sir.'

'Thank you, Roger.' A priestly smile, a little benediction for the eager acolyte.

At the connecting-door Wesley paused with his fingers curled about the brass knob.

'Is it done to ask how Paris went, sir? This Peterson chap?'

Well – no; it wasn't done; but a loaf had to be rewarded with at least a crumb.

Coast rubbed his finger and thumb together in the age-old gesture of the market-place.

'In our pockets, Roger. Absolutely. You can read the memo.'

Quilter busied himself at the tipple-cabinet. The soft grumble of traffic along Whitehall drifted in through the open window.

'Can we trust him, do you think?'

'A double, Tony? Can one ever?'

'But as a double working for the same side; is that quite the same?' Quilter came away from the cabinet with two crystal glasses. 'I mean in your opinion.'

Coast shrugged.

'His alternative is to work for the other side. I think he's too cautious for that.'

Peterson had worn caution like a badge. His fear of being followed and overheard had been so obsessive that he and Coast had held the last meeting of their protracted negotiations in the rain in the Père Lachaise cemetery. Peterson had even quartered the area first, ostensibly looking for a particular tomb. He had chain smoked, grinding out one cigarette after another in the wet grass. At sixty, and with his pension almost due, Peterson was not a man to take chances.

'Four thousand a quarter, Swiss. The Treasury won't like that.'

'He won't work for less, Tony. – Expensive young wife.'

Roma Peterson had been the unexpected bonus. At first a way in to probe out Peterson's weaknesses; but later the bonus. He rarely took the risk of dropping *crottes* on his own doorstep; but she was in Paris, and before the end of the year would be safely back in Connecticut and setting up house for Peterson's retirement. There were plenty of tightly trousered little French boys to fill in her time till then.

'And how does he contact us?'

'The personal-column of the Telegraph.' Coast made a nod towards the memo on Quilter's desk. 'It's all logged in there.'

Quilter plainly had doubts. He said abruptly:

'I'm not altogether sure that I like the idea of your being his control, Jocelyn.'

Coast's sherry paused fractionally on its way to his mouth. The quality of Quilter's sherry improved in direct proportion to the approach of his KBE. Perhaps he had already got it. He looked unsettled about something this morning.

'Oh, no offence, Jocelyn. But it's a courier's job. Boy's work. Young Wesley for instance. You are the Deputy Head of Section, after all.'

'Face to face, Tony. He insists. No middle-men.'

He and Quilter had always used Christian names. They had known each other, on and off, for almost their lifetime, and it still irked Coast that he had to owe at least his outward allegiance to a contemporary whom he better remembered as a snivelling little oick at preparatory-school. They had come together later at Oxford, where Quilter had got a Second to Coast's First. Quilter's work had rarely been better than pedestrian.

'Reasonable I suppose.'

Quilter had sprawled back in his chair and tried to look at ease, but his left hand worked incessantly at crumbling invisible bread and that was always a sign to the contrary. There was definitely something on his mind this morning, certainly something more than the subornment of Gus Peterson. At one point, glancing up, he met Coast's eye and started to open his mouth; but then clearly changed his mind again.

He said instead, 'Mingay's delighted, of course, – and it goes without saying – I hold you personally in the highest regard ... '

Coast waited; bullshit like that was usually a preamble to an invitation to lunch at Quilter's awful mausoleum of a club where Quilter was on the committee. Quilter wasn't half the man Foster had been. His overly protuberant eyes were brought about by some sort of chronic thyroid condition for which he occasionally had injections; only Coast, and Quilter and his doctor knew that.

'I thought perhaps lunch – a little celebration.'

At his awful mausoleum of a club; and Coast had to twist the lower half of his face into a semblance of a smile and say:

'Civil of you, Tony. Look forward to it.'

He was back behind his desk at a quarter to three, and broaching a packet of Rennies from its cellophane outer wrappings when Claire Goldring knocked and stalked in. She had been seconded from the Treasury a few months ago, when Mrs. Copeland had retired; and as Lomax had observed, in one of his more leerily crapulous moments, at the present exchange-rate for gilt-edged centrefold material he was surprised that the Treasury had handed her over without any sort of collateral.

'Your Dutch project, Mr. Coast. For checking.'

The bluest eyes, a tall, luxurious figure. He had been tempted himself, but too many others had succumbed to similar velvet traps and had been caught by the short hairs.

'And it will be immaculate, of course.'

A tight, glacial smile; she rarely gave more. A way, he supposed, of protecting her priceless virginity.

Her father was a Group-Captain, one of her uncles on the permanent supply-staff of NATO in Brussels. She had crossed the street with impeccable references.

'The draft's inside,' she said. ' – And while you were away there was a new instruction about shredding drafts – .'

'Yes, I've seen it, Miss Goldring,' he broke in. 'Thank you.'

Toler had tried, and so had Wesley before the advent of the angular Miss Spencer. So far, it appeared, Miss Goldring was impregnable.

'Thank you, Miss Goldring.'

She flicked him a glance that might have been inimical. Then turned on a heel and stalked out again, a certain

stiffness in her walk because she knew he was watching her.
His interest faded as soon as she had gone.
What she had left behind, a slender report bound in a yellow plastic cover with a Top Secret sticker splashed diagonally across its upper corner, these weightless few sheets of paper, represented most of the Section's work for the previous three months; a detailed summary of the latest state of the Royal Netherlands Air Force, its command structure, the disposition, strengths and strike values of its various squadrons, its budget, its condition of readiness and its state of morale; a document so sensitive that even the Netherlands Air Staff across at the Hague was totally unaware of its existence. Coast had been the project's co-ordinator, the sorter of wheat from chaff and facts from fictions, and paymaster to several high ranking Dutch Air-officers who saw no crime in selling to their allies what they would never sell to the KGB at any price. Doubtless a similar document outlining the gapes and rents in the Royal Air Force of the United Kingdom lay on a similar desk in Washington or Bonn or wherever. Even in NATO the practice was common; the trusted overseen by the even more trusted.

At six o'clock the westering sun poured liquid gold across the rooftops of St. James's and sparkled off the myriad windows of the distant Hilton.
With the taste of fear already brewing in his mouth, metallic, like copper, he put on his jacket and switched off his desk-lamp. In the office next door young Wesley was also going through the motions of battening down the hatches for the night and out in the corridor a floor-polisher whined softly as the cleaners began on their evening business. Of habit, he glanced around once; desk, cabinet, safe; all secure, calendar set for tomorrow.
And of habit, again, he gave his office door a thump with the heel of his hand after he had locked it. He skirted the polishing machine.
'Goodnight.'

' 'Night, sir.'

A small word for everyone. It paid.

He reached the landing just as the lift purred up and its doors hissed open with a gasp of pheumatics. Miss Goldring was just stepping into it.

He had hoped to have the lift to himself. Always at the back of his mind lay the idea that fear might also have a special face.

'Forget to go home, Miss Goldring?'

She was going to a concert. It hadn't been worth going home and then coming back again, so she had stayed on for half an hour.

The lift was hot and claustrophobic. He felt like hooking a finger behind his shirt-collar and loosening it, but he stayed the need. The coppery taste filled his mouth. The one thing Borisenko had not warned him about that day was fear, the physical symptoms of it; the way it dried the mouth and twisted the gut.

The lift jerked to a stop and he remembered just in time to usher her out ahead of him.

From one of the ground floor offices came the intermittent clatter of a telex machine.

There was an extra security-man on duty tonight, and Goldring passed some pithy comment about lightning striking twice in the one place; and he remembered Wesley telling him about how she had had her handbag gone through on Friday evening. So there was a temporary tightening of security. It wouldn't last; it never did. A week, and everyone would decide that the new procedures were no more effective than the old ones. But today, of all days ...

One of the two guards – Sam, yes, his name was Sam – daughter – wedding – Majorca – straightened up from the racing-pages the two of them were hunched over and stepped out from behind the reception-desk to bar their way.

He touched the glossy black visor of his cap apologetically.

'I beg your pardon, Mr. Coast, sir; Miss. Spot security-check. It's orders I'm afraid. You're not taking any work home? Files, that sort of thing?'

Or a handwritten draft, which ought to have been consigned to the shredder in the Registry – he had fed in old rubbish instead – copiously detailing the present standing and strike values of the Royal Netherlands Air Force, together with a list of all the Dutch officers who had illictly subscribed to it.

His hand became sticky about the handle of his briefcase; there had never been a body-search in all the years, but it was a possibility of which he never ceased to be aware.

It was Goldring, however, who was the more flustered. Coast it was, the professional, who covered his spurt of alarm with an actor's bravura, opening his briefcase with a flourish and pulling out a Daily Telegraph and an Amateur Photographer and his collapsible umbrella and making some hearty joke about horses and stable doors and which a moment later he could not remember.

And then Whitehall, the swing-doors flapping behind him and the reek of petrol fumes.

In the blacked-out bathroom, he stripped the exposed length of 35-millimetre film out of its cassette, re-rolled it into a tight spiral again then slipped it into a cylindrical aluminium container of much the same size as the cassette. He brushed his hand lightly along the window-sill to find the cap, fumbled it into position, then screwed it down.

The light momentarily dazzled him when he switched it on again. He checked the cap on the canister to make sure that it was light-tight. It purported to contain Aldomet tablets to reduce blood pressure – dispensed to a Mr. J.A. Petrie, two tablets three times a day – and bore the label of a reputable chemist in the Strand. Anyone finding a film cassette would know exactly what it was; a drug box that felt empty would more than likely be opened – and the film would cease to be evidence the moment the light struck it.

He put away his cotton gloves and his camera, and put the container into the pocket of the jacket he intended to wear tomorrow. It was eleven o'clock. Photographing the twenty or so sheets of A4 had taken him the best part of an hour.

Then, methodically, he ripped the draft, sheet by sheet, into minute shreds and took them into the lavatory to soak in the pan while he showered and shaved, then flushed them away. An hour, at most, and they would be indistinguishable from the rest of the liquid detritus swilling around the sewage system of south-west London.

With a bathrobe sashed about him, he poured himself a whisky, a large one. He always kept several bottles about the place, bought them in pubs and off-licenses and supermarkets so that he was not marked down in any one place as a heavy drinker.

He took it down in two swallows, hot and biting, then poured himself another while he waited for the reaction to come now that the job was finished. At one time he could take the tension in his stride. He no longer could.

The flat seemed to shrink a little each day, and even with the windows flung wide there seemed to be no air. He watched the traffic four floors below. He had chosen to live on Streatham Hill for its anonymity. His possessions were few and if he left the place tomorrow, exactly as it was, there was nothing here to judge him by, no stamp of character. His furniture was of good quality, but sparse, the bric-a-brac ordinary and there was only one photograph, and that of his younger self taken with the rest of a rowing-eight at Oxford. With his approaching floridity now he could have been any one of them. This was the sleeping place of a man ready at any moment to up sticks and take himself off.

The shakes were coming on. When he raised his glass it chattered against his lower teeth. He was getting old, past it. In three years he would be fifty.

It was at Oxford that Nikky Borisenko had sought him out. Half a lifetime ago, almost to the day. It seemed longer. A hundred years.

They had sat on the bank of Christchurch Meadow. Borisenko had tossed pebbles into the river, making, with the first one, a circular target of ripples into which he lazily aimed the remainder of the stones cupped in his right hand.

Young Jocelyn Coast had watched the stones, the way they caught and sparkled back the sunlight. A golden girl with the finely drawn muscles of an athlete skimmed by in a college skiff. He remembered seeing everything that day with a new and heightened acuity. They had found out somehow that he was destined for the Foreign Service. And they had sought him out. And he was flattered.

He must not appear ambitious. They already had men at the top – and too many men at the very bottom – more men were needed in the middle, intelligent men, interceptors of gossip of every kind. Who was homosexual, lesbian, deviate, alchoholic. Who was weak, who was strong, who knew who, who needed money to pay debts.

They rose, they walked. Not yet thirty himself, Borisenko walked already with an old man's stoop.

– And the trick is to be sociable, but not thrusting. Always stay at the outer fringes of the crowd, that way it is easier to see exactly who is standing behind you.

Treading through the grass, they might have been don and pupil.

No man was of much use to them before he was thirty-five. It took a man ten years to establish himself, to insinuate himself, and win the right kind of confidences. For a few years, he must not be surprised if they did not contact him at all. During that time he would be as valuable to them as he would be later on. He would be observed, but never the observer. They would be monitoring his progress; and then, one day, out of the blue, they would again make contact with him. A chance meeting on a bus or in a train or in a restaurant, or even by telephone. The man's name would be Michael. And Coast would be Anthony. The conversation would be unambiguous. Mention would be made of this very conversation by the river, the exact date and even the weather.

And if anything should ever go wrong – pfft! – a noisy click of finger and thumb breaking the lovely stillness of a Sunday afternoon – like that, we shall spirit you away. So fast that your people back here will wonder if you had even existed at all, or if they had merely imagined you.

Pfft! – like that, we shall spirit you away, Jocelyn. We *always* look after our own. For more than twenty-three years Coast had carried that sound and those words in his head. They were his crucifix, his talisman.

But Borisenko had never warned him of the fear that Sunday afternoon. The way it came like a sudden twist of a knife in the gut, the way it shrivelled the scrotum and stretched the arm for the whisky-bottle at ever-diminishing intervals.

He woke in the blackest hours between the wolf and the dog, not surfacing but starting out of sleep in an ice-cold sweat of fear from a dream in which he had been standing knee-deep amid a pile of papers he had stolen; while a security-guard frisked him for more and his mother – long dead – stood by in one of her Ascot hats and told him what a stupid boy he was. This last was from life, which had lent the dream its appalling reality.

The cigarette he lit tasted foul and metallic.

He was like a man on a runaway roundabout. There had been one last moment when he might have jumped clear and escaped unscathed. If he jumped now he would be dashed to pieces. Borisenko was long gone and left him to the mercy of the Michaels. Michael One, Michael Two, Michael Three. In the twelve years of the dynasty – the first had made contact in the summer of 'seventy-one – there had been six of them, four known by sight, the other two only voices over a telephone who guarded their mysteries like a woman. These days he saw only couriers, a man or a woman, who wore a bow-tie and carried a certain document-case with the stamped metal letters JA beside the pull of the zip fastener.

When the alarm buzzed at seven o'clock he awoke as if he had not slept at all. Like most men who live alone he breakfasted with the least possible effort, a slice of toast and marmalade, two cups of coffee, a cigarette – or two – or three. At half-past seven he dialled a number on the

Battersea exchange. He listened for the telephone at the other end to ring six times, then hung up. He did this again at a quarter to eight and again at eight o'clock. His own telephone rang six times at five past eight. He did not answer it.

At ten to nine he was standing beside the chocolate vending-machine on the east-bound platform of Victoria Underground station. The platform drained and filled again as the trains clattered in. He had seen three come and go and there was still no sign of the courier. Several times he had furtively touched his pocket to check that the aluminium pill-box was still there.

The platform filled again. It was eight minutes to nine. That copper taste again, impossible to swallow.

Another train. When it went out he was alone on the platform.

A river of passengers gushed through the arch beside him from a train on one of the other platforms. His eyes swept anxiously over it. A black-bow tie; a brown plastic document-case with brass letters JA beside the pull of the zip fastener. A woman he hadn't seen before. Probably a typist from Kensington Palace Gardens. The longer he worked for them, the more contemptibly they seemed to treat him.

They tried to close with each other but there were too many people in the way.

There was a gust of cooler air, a crashing roar, a sudden eruption of lights.

Coast and the woman battled forward into the press and gradually funnelled together. He felt her hand take a tight grip on the tail of his jacket as he stepped into the already crowded carriage. They shared a strap. He could smell her perfume and the heat rising from her. She wore the sort of lipstick that looks glossily and unpleasantly adhesive.

The train didn't start at once. For two or three minutes there was silence, broken occasionally by the rustle of a newspaper and the clearing of a throat. It was another stifling morning and the smell and closeness of humankind about him was suffocating. A couple of hundred people all jammed into the same metal box and sharing the same few cubic feet of stale air. He loathed the Tube. Some mornings he couldn't face it at all and took a bus.

Then mercifully the motors purred and the vacuum-brakes hissed off.

They made the pass a few seconds before St. James's Park. As the brakes went on they were rammed together. Her document case appeared to slip; he appeared to catch it. There was a moment of seeming confusion with the case trapped between them. As the pill-box went from hand to hand one of her fingernails scraped across his wrist.

As the train slowed she tucked the case back beneath her arm.

'Thank you,' she said. 'I am so sorry.'

As soon as the train stopped he was off it and thrusting his way up to the daylight and fresh air of Petty France.

Three

The weather became more relentless, and the Saturday of that week was hot enough to dull the senses and turn all the bodily saps to a sluggishly flowing treacle.

He stopped off in Sevenoaks soon after ten. He bought a luxuriant bouquet of pink freesias, a small flask of Arpèges, a Dunlop tennis racquet and six yellow balls, an encyclopaedia on handguns and a plastic and metal kit of a Walther PPK pistol that looked horribly real if the picture on the box lid was anything to go by. He did not so much select as plunder, and was back in the car with his shirt sticking to his back well inside twenty minutes.

He was in Southborough by a quarter to eleven and canting the Volvo up on the grass verge in front of the cottage. The woodwork looked freshly painted and an aluminium gutter around the eaves had replaced the leaking iron one that had started to fall apart at Christmas during the snow.

He reached over to the back seat for the flowers and the perfume, the tennis racquet and the encyclopaedia. The plastic kit, he decided, was too overtly a bribe; best see first how the land lay.

He climbed out and with full arms managed to lock the car door. He hated coming here. He could never make an entrance without feeling he'd got his tail between his legs, and was an interloper.

As he barged through the front gate she was waiting for him on the flagged path that led around to the back of the cottage. She was in a red shirt, a pair of tailored black slacks. She had never been anything less than smart.

'Frances.'

'Joss.'

'You look fine.'

'And you don't.'

She made no move to help him with his balancing act, except to hold the gate open and stand aside for him.

'To what do we owe the privilege?'

'I did ring.'

'But not last month.'

'I was busy. I'm sorry.'

She fixed him with cold eyes. Liar, they said.

She had had a concrete patio built on at the back, with white tubs on it brimming with flowers.

She received his flowers with grace, although he felt foolish when he saw how the garden was flooded with them. She had always been able to grow anything, once a miniature orange tree, from a pip, in a pot on the window sill of the flat they had had in Athens.

' – And this.' The bottle of Arpèges. ' – And don't worry, it's not a peace offering. Consider it the price of lunch.'

On the patio there had been a wrought-iron table set for lunch, a sheet of muslin over it to keep the flies away. To his disappointment, it had been set only for three.

'No Simon?' he asked.

'No, I'm sorry. He's spending the weekend across at Sevenoaks. He has a little girlfriend.'

'At sixteen?'

'They grow up faster these days – especially when they're out of sight.'

They were back to the old *tu quoque*. He refused to bite. It was not one of his pithy days and he had come unarmed.

'Where's Dizzy?'

'Shopping. Last minute odds and ends. You didn't give us much notice.'

He had 'phoned last night, Friday, late; on a sudden lonely whim.

'I presume you'd like a drink. A whisky is it – still?'
'Please. A small one.'

Perversely, she poured him a large one. From a bottle of Haig that was already half-empty. The last time he had been here she had served him Black and White from a new bottle. And he had already observed the started packet of cigarettes and the chunky silver lighter beside the clock. Left behind; not hers. And she hadn't even taken the trouble to hide them.

'Cheers.'

'Ciao.' She took a token sip of her sherry – she had never been a drinker – then left him to his own devices while she went to put his flowers in water.

The furniture he remembered. The divorce, after all the clawing and biting, had been surprisingly amicable, the house sold, the proceeds equally divided. She had asked for no money except for the children's school fees. He had been granted access to them once a fortnight, and for a few months he had visited regularly and taken them out; but then he had found another woman – he needed women the way other men needed air and light – and gradually lapsed. During the last three years he could count his visits on his fingers.

She came back after a few minutes with his flowers in a china vase.

'You can sit down.'

He lowered himself awkwardly to the edge of an armchair, she opposite, each of them aware of how precarious this all was, a couple of yards of hearthrug between them like a no-man's land bristling with booby-traps. She looked well. A new venture into brighter war-paint, a slick sleek hairstyle. At forty-three she could have passed for a well-preserved thirty-five.

'How are you, Frances?'

She sketched a shrug.

'Oh, not bad.'

'And the children?'

'Fighting fit. Simon's just taken his O-levels. Sweating on

the results.'

Silence, a beat or two of it. A trapped fly buzzed frenziedly between the net curtain and the glass of the open french-door before making its escape into the garden.

'How are the Lomaxes?' she asked.

'Fine,' he replied. She had always liked Lomax and his wife. During the early days in Athens, Lomax and Katerina had been their mentors.

Another silence, thick and palpable. In Athens once they had made love against the bathroom wall. Two other people, that had been. They had met at Oxford, and married the week before he was posted to Athens. It had taken him ten years to realise that marriage and his extra-territorial needs for reassurance and his deep political commitment were all mutually exclusive. She knew about the women, but of the darker side of his life she knew nothing. She was apolitical in those days, and he had never tried to make her understand that government by consent was merely Fascism in disguise. It was his pride that he had never taken money for what he did, which was why he was able to despise petty little bourgeois backsliders like Peterson, and fools like Quilter.

There was nothing to say, nothing here at all for him. Last night, with four walls closing in and another weekend towering insurmountably in front of him, in a moment of mental aberration and a haze of alcoholic sentimentality, he had thought there might have been.

It was with relief that he heard the loosely metallic sounds of a bicycle being dismounted and leaned against the wall by the open back door, the rustling of paper in the kitchen, the door of the refrigerator being opened and then closed, the light hurrying footsteps along the hall.

'Hello, Daddy.'

Darker than her mother. Little high heels and tight jeans and just a trace of lipstick. Another year and she would be some pimpled yob's first glimpse over the wall into Paradise. Hips, and trim little bust.

She flew to kiss him. He scarcely had time to rise and swing his glass out of the way.

'Hello, Dizzy. How are you?'

All the platitudes. He said she was pretty; but she already knew, he could see.

Over lunch she chatted incessantly, about school, her friends, and he was aware several times of her crudely overt attempts to draw he and Frances into the same conversation. And that also she was flirting with him in a way that was faintly incestuous and that he was enjoying it and that Frances disapproved; and that when Frances sent her in for the strawberries she was about to deliver the death-blow.

Which she did.

'I'm getting married again, Joss,' she said.

A tight hand came about his viscera.

'Congratulations. Anyone I know?' Too flippant.

The cold eyes fixed him again. It was not a moment for banter.

'That was crass,' he said. 'I'm sorry.'

He was the senior lecturer in mathematics at the college where she was the bursar.

'It's been going on for some time,' she said. 'He's a widower. No children. He has a home, and Simon gets on well with him – Dizzy, of course, doesn't. We thought the first week in August. I'd prefer that the children visited you after that. If that's acceptable.'

She managed to make it all sound even more final than the divorce had been.

'Yes, of course,' he said. ' – And I am pleased, Frances. Really.'

Susan – Dizzy – it was a name she had coined for herself when she was too young to wrap her tongue around Susie – played a fierce game of tennis. In the old days it was only pat-ball and he had always contrived to let her beat him. Now it was the other way round. And afterwards, happily, sweatily, tasting of salt, she had kissed him again.

In the evening he drove her into Tunbridge Wells and wined her and dined her in a romantic little lair of alcoves and bottle bottom windows. She was in a too-short pretty dress and white tights and high heels and wore her hair loose. She made him feel a hundred years old.

Spandau Ballet, The Police; he only remembered the Beatles. Christ, she hadn't even been born then.

'I think you're getting squiffy,' he said.

She grinned. Lovely white young teeth. 'Only a little bit. And I rather like it. But I won't be sick, I promise.'

It made his stomach screw up just to look at her. He had long forgotten what innocence was, or even if he had ever been possessed of it.

'Perhaps you'd like to come up to Town one evening. Stay the night. We'll take in a Prom.'

Her eyes sparkled. It may have been just the wine, but he didn't think so.

'Super. Love to. When?'

He had not really expected her to take him up on it. He had let the children down so often that he could scarcely credit any belief they still had in his fatherly integrity.

'Soon.' Not good enough. Too vague. He had seen the brief flicker of disappointment. 'Next month. – I'll get tickets and give you a ring. – And send Mummy a cheque for a new dress.' This time he would. God help him, he meant it.

He drove her back at midnight.

'The witching hour,' he said.

'It's been lovely, Daddy. Really. – Do you want to come in for coffee or anything?'

'Better not. Mummy's waiting up. Mustn't put her out.'

She put up her face and kissed him, not a child's kiss, but savagely, with a hand at his waist to twist him close. When he drew away, he knew that never again must he let her kiss him like that. In the half dark he could see the glint of hooded eyes and perhaps a realisation too on her part that each of them had gone too far.

'I do love you, Daddy.'

He heard the small choked rattle in her throat, a sound heard all too often before in seedier circumstances with other women.

'I know you do, Dizzy. – I love you too.'

'– Has Mummy told you; about Donald?'

'The duck?'

'It's not funny, Daddy.' She regarded him gravely in the dark. 'We're going to live with him, Mummy says. – Simon wants to. I don't.'

'I have to be neutral – do you know what that means?'

She hung her head.

'Yes, I know what it means. Sorry, Daddy.'

She fiddled with the little evening-bag on her lap.

'– And I'm sorry Simon wasn't here,' she said. 'I don't think he means it. Honestly.'

'It's all right, darling. I know how he feels. I don't blame him. – I'll give Mummy a buzz about the Proms. Promise.'

Another kiss, this time an impulsive one as he leaned across to open the door for her.

'I love you, Daddy.'

'You too, darling.'

He drew the door quietly to and watched her clack a little unsteadily up the path to the front door and sort out her latch-key. She turned and waved. He raised a hand.

He drove back too carelessly and too fast. A few miles along the motorway, in the mirror, he glimpsed a flashing blue light hard on his tail. He was pulling over into the slow lane, his excuses and apologies all ready and hoping to Christ they wouldn't breathylise him, when the white Land-Rover rocketed by on his off-side, light still flashing, siren wailing. They were not after him; but the experience was salutory enough to make him cut his speed down to forty and keep it there.

He came upon the accident a few miles further on; a car askew against a buckled length of safety-fence, a huddled leather-clad body on the central reservation, the antiseptic white inside of an ambulance, a distorted motor-cycle on its side.

He tried not to look too closely, but saw it all too clearly from the tail of his eye despite himself. He had never been drawn to violence.

A motorway policeman in an orange overjacket waved

him by, his silhouette huge against the floodlight from the white Land-Rover.

He drove cautiously after that, feeling queasy, and more aware than for a long time of his own mortality.

Four

Coast sank his single whisky and ordered another. He sank six each evening between the station at Streatham Hill and his flat; two singles here, two at the next port of call and two at the last. If there had been four public houses on the way he would have doubtless have sunk eight single whiskies. Afterwards there was the private bottle and the winding down from Monday in order to gird himself for Tuesday, Wednesday, Thursday and Friday.

He exchanged another speculative smile with the smartly dressed young brunette further along the bar. She had already turned through ninety degrees on her stool to make the semaphores clearer, the frequent rearranging of the legs, the slow-burn looks when her tee-shirted and be-jeaned escort had his nose in his beer jug, and the occasional return of the speculative smile. The unwashed escort, in hind view, exuded a muscular sexuality, but the girl was possibly in the market for something more subtle.

Not that Coast could afford the risk, but it was gratifying to know that he could still pull an attractive piece of stray and that his own biological response had not gone away for ever. Soon there would be no sensation at all, only the cold black void, the eternal blank, The thought terrified him.

But then the muscular backside took itself off to the toilets and the girl turned back to face the counter and used the stack of change he had ostentatiously left behind to buy another round. Her face was impassive. For her it had only been a game.

*

He whisked an omelette together and caught the tailpieces of the ten o'clock news on the television. They were still scrapping it out in the Middle East; another oil-rig was about to go on-stream in the North Sea. The balances of payments had, but only just; and the grand total of the unemployed had been adjusted downward again by the crude manipulation of statistics.

He fretfully switched it off. The visit to Southborough on Saturday had left him with an adolescent resentment which he had tried to shrug away, but had so far not succeeded in doing. There had been Frances' news, young Simon's not being there; the new guttering; and the fresh lick of paint, probably lovingly applied by the shadowy Donald, and Susan kissing him with such savage desperation that he had felt the sharpness of her teeth. And, just as ridiculously, more fuel had been added by the brunette in the bar suddenly turning it all off. Not that he had wanted her, but he had played the game by the rules and she had not. It all felt like a conspiracy.

He was in the kitchen when the telephone rang, washing his plate and cutlery and frying-pan. He kept to a strict regime about things like that; in the early days after the divorce he had let everything slide to the brink and only pulled himself together when it was almost too late. He counted the rings.

... Five

... six

... seven

... it wasn't Michael, thank God ... eight ... and it wouldn't be Frances ... ten ... Susan.

For no good reason he suddenly felt sure it was Susan, perhaps to thank him again for Saturday; she did sometimes, several days afterwards, and he went quickly to answer the strident summons before she rang off.

'Hello?'

'Joss?'

It was a voice that did not immediately make a picture form. A woman; but over the last few years there had been half a dozen of them, each one little different from the one before, all blurred together and indistinguishable.

'I'm sorry?' he said, plastering on a smile because even over the telephone a smile had a special sound, and any woman at all who took the trouble to telephone was a woman in hand.

A fat, earthy chuckle rattled tinnily in the earpiece.

'Oh, come on, Joss. You know just who it is – .'

He did. The stretched vowels, the nasal twang. And sounding close enough to be just around the corner.

'... Roma. How are you?'

'Oh, you can do better than that. You sound as if your teeth are gritted together. I thought I'd give you a surprise.'

'You did.' Already the comfortable feeling was seeping into his viscera. He was always at his best with a woman. 'A delicious sound. I've missed it.' He heard a lighter snap open, a quick inhalation.

'Go on,' she said. 'I'm still listening.'

' – And you too, of course.'

Another of the chuckles that were aimed for the groin, and that tonight, the way he felt, homed unerringly on to target.

'Better. Although I'm still not sure I believe you. I had to get your number out of Gus's little black book. You forgot to leave it with me.'

So Gus Peterson was stupid as well as neurotic.

'Surely not. I made sure I had. Sorry.'

She sounded clear enough to be in London; but she was still in Paris, and when he asked how she was, again, she spent a tedious few minutes telling him. In Paris, towards the end, she had become a bore, a momentary diversion that was best forgotten, but he found himself talking back to her in all the old well-tried ways. During all the years she had been his only venture in combining business with pleasure, and he knew all too well the danger of that; but he needed a woman, for sex, for spite, for reassurance; and she was coming to London.

'I've persuaded Gus I need some new clothes. I thought I

might fly over for a few days.'

'Why only a few days?'

'You know Gus. Mean as they come.'

'Arrange it around a weekend,' he said. For these occasions, as well as the portfolio of stratagems, there was also a special voice. It was soft, persuasive. 'We could get together ... '

'Yes. That'd be great.' Her voice too had softened. 'Look, hon, I'll try for the Thursday morning flight – give you a ring on Thursday evening.'

He could hear her breathing, and in the background a muted voice speaking French either on a television or a radio.

'And I'll have something fixed for Friday evening. – We'll play it by ear after that.'

'Yes,' she said. 'Do that.'

She hung on for a long time, talking of what she had bought for herself, of how dreary Gus was, of how she and a friend had almost allowed themselves to be picked up earlier that evening in a little restaurant near the Ronde Point out of sheer bloody boredom. And listening to her made plain Peterson's need to supplement whatever salary it was that the CIA paid him. With her clothes, trips abroad, her telephone bills and her taxis she was probably bleeding the stupid bastard white.

Then she became sentimental again, talked of the week in Paris, that little *pension* they'd gone to that afternoon and made love in behind the drawn curtains, then gone to that place at the bottom of the steps up to the Sacré Coeur, then returned to the *pension* for the night because Gus had gone out of town on business. And then the sentiment and the sex became confused with the more permanent attachments between a man and a woman, and Coast had to skirmish more cautiously; and when the line at last went dead, he was left with the distinct feeling that he had said too much and that Roma Peterson might possibly become a nuisance.

*

An open office door was always an invitation to Eric Lomax.

With a file in one hand he flapped the other in a feeble Roman salute.

'All hail, old boy,' he said, then peered around the office, then, like a ham actor playing detective, behind the door. Lomax had one of those unfortunate faces where most of the underlying flesh at the top appears to have sagged to the bottom, and fallen into flews, so that whatever expression he wore was always partially concealed behind the mask of a doleful bloodhound. 'Busy?'

'Not particularly,' replied Coast. 'You?'

'In the doldrums, old boy. Totally becalmed.'

Coast shoved his cigarette-casket forward, and Lomax came the last few paces between the door and the desk, breasting the air like a sweaty and overfed pasha, and slumped wearily into the spare chair. His waistcoat was unbuttoned, his necktie loosened and there were moist dark patches about the armpits of his shirt.

He lit a cigarette with a tremulous hand, and exhaled on a long tired breath. His broad, raked-back forehead was beaded with perspiration.

'How's that lovely girl of yours? Seen her lately?'

'Last week-end. She's fine. Sends her regards.'

Lomax sprawled with his heavy legs outstretched, and his swag belly framed by a pair of red braces and the tight waistband of his black trousers. Long gone was the tall slim man with the pretty Greek wife who had had the apartment in Georgiadis Street and kept open house to all and sundry who cared to call; among them a stripling boy freshly recruited into the Diplomatic Service, and his new young wife. At fifty-nine he was falling to pieces, almost with deliberation.

'And how's Kat?'

'Very understanding, bless her. Still thinks the sun shines out of me.'

They shunted the weather about, then the wedding of Wesley and Miss Spencer. But it was clear that there was more on Lomax's mind than the temperature and Wesley's nuptials, although he was a long time getting around to whatever it was.

A document-trolley with a squeaky wheel went by in the direction of the Registry. When the sound of it had finally receded, Lomax's mournful eyes peered through a veil of cigarette smoke.

'What do you know about a *cordon sanitaire*, old boy?'

'Around what?'

'Me, old boy.'

Coast spread his hands.

'Riddles, Eric. Haven't a clue what you're talking about.'

The mournful eyes became reproachful.

'Pity. I thought you might.'

Coast leaned back tiredly in his chair. The air was hot and muggy and unmoving, and these days Lomax rambled more than was good for him.

'I'm sorry,' he said. 'I don't.'

Lomax sat there, sweatily, measuring him over the desk.

'Look, old boy,' he said at length, very quietly. 'I know I'm presuming on an old friendship – and I know you're a good few grades up the ladder from me nowadays – but I'd like a few minutes with you; off parade. I'm sure there's something going on in this bloody place, and I want to know about it.'

Coast had an armoury of excuses to hand, but whatever problem Eric Lomax had, or was imagining, was clearly of great importance to him; or, and which was more important to Coast, Lomax had latched on to something going on in the Section that Coast did not know about.

'One o'clock,' he proposed. 'That suit you? Meet you in the Threshers.'

Lomax looked immeasurably relieved.

'Thanks, old boy. Greatly obliged to you.' He levered himself ponderously out of the chair and took up the red file he had brought in. Then grinding out his cigarette with more concentration than was strictly necessary, he looked down and across at Coast from under his eyebrows.

'See you in the Threshers. Don't let me down, will you old boy?'

At one o'clock Lomax was already anchored to the crowded bar with a large vodka in his hand.

'What'll you have, old boy?'

'Scotch, Eric. Small one.'

Lomax sorted out coins and arranged them on the counter. His movements were the slow studied ones of the determined drinker. When the drinks came, he took a sip of the vodka he already had, then tipped the one he had just bought into the same glass.

'Cheers, old boy.'

'Cheers. – Going it a bit, aren't you, Eric; double-doubles? At lunchtime?'

Lomax looked guiltily down into his glass, then up again.

'Is that a warning, old chap? – As Section Dep.?'

'Just trying to do you a favour.'

Lomax smiled wryly.

'Shall have to watch myself, then, shan't I, old boy. Hadn't realised I was reeling so obviously.'

They found a table in a corner by the Space Invaders machine. Lomax proffered a crumpled pack of Gauloises.

'No thanks. Prefer my own.'

Lomax fumbled in his waistcoat for his lighter, lit his cigarette with a wavering hand, then was racked with a fit of coughing.

He smote his chest with the edge of his fist, his eyes still watering. Much of Lomax was a lapsed actor.

'Knackered,' he wheezed. 'Bloody well knackered. Bloody fags and bloody booze – and I've just caught myself looking at little schoolgirls in long white socks by way of sexual gratification. Fifty-nine years old, and I've finally reached the bottom of the heap.' Lomax twitched in another burst of silent coughing, and when that was over dabbed the perspiration from his flabby face with the handkerchief he kept up his sleeve. 'Take heed, old boy,' he said, as he stuffed the handkerchief back again. 'There, but for the grace of God, go you.' He was silent for a moment as he reached out for his vodka and took a heavy swig of it.

'Does Kat know you're knocking the stuff back like that?'

Lomax's face crumpled into a sad smile.

'Ah – my little Greek. Yes, she knows. We've got this little game; she hides the bloody bottles and I have to try and find 'em again.'

Almost all that remained of the quadruple vodka went down at a swallow. Coast watched with distaste.

'She still loves me, though, old boy. Hard to believe, eh?'

'Not entirely,' replied Coast. 'I know Kat.'

'Yes,' said Lomax, his face briefly crumpling again. 'So you do.'

What was harder to believe was that this obese caricature of a man sitting opposite had once been both a soldier and a scholar. During the war, he had been parachuted into Crete to lead a band of partisans working out of the mountains, and even under his alcoholic veneer now was an educated man who spoke Greek like an Athenian and Turkish like a bazaar-trader. Lomax looked after the eastern end of the Mediterranean, so far with competence, although Quilter had made one or two spiky comments of late about the quality of his reports. As a member of the Section he pre-dated both Quilter and Coast by several years and had worked under the immediate aegis of Foster during the chilliest days of the Cold War.

The Space Invaders machine beeped and spluttered, and Lomax still did not come to the point until there was another vodka in front of him and he lit another cigarette from the stub of the last.

'What I want to know, old boy,' he said, hunched forward confidentially over the stained table, 'Is who, since last Friday afternoon at five o'clock, has drawn the little black ball out of the draw-string bag, and scored the line through the name of Lomax.'

Today was only Wednesday. And, so far as Coast was concerned, the last two and a half working days had produced nothing out of the ordinary.

'You're getting maudlin, Eric,' he said. 'Snap out of it. It doesn't suit you.'

Lomax looked solemnly back. His third vodka stood so far untouched.

'But you do know what I'm talking about, don't you, old boy?'

'I haven't the faintest idea.'

Lomax held up four splayed fingers and folded them down one at a time.

'The telexes that don't land on my desk any more, unless they've been given the once-over by Quilter; the files that don't seem to be in the Registry when I want them; the way Heatherington hangs about when I'm using the Xerox machine to make sure that I only make the number of copies I sign for.' The solitary little finger stayed poised to wag. 'I tell you, old boy; it's all too bloody obvious, too sudden.'

If all this were true, it was news. But what was more probable was that Lomax was imagining it. In two and a half days a hint, at least, would have filtered down from Quilter. Nothing had.

Coast shook his head.

'I still don't know what you're talking about.'

The melancholy eyes no longer were. There was suddenly in them a trace of the old Lomax, astute and watchful.

'It's true, old boy. In a few days I've gone from trusty old servant to *persona non* bloody *grata*.' Lomax hunched closer. He still hadn't picked up the third vodka. A whoop of triumph came from the group around the Space Invader console. 'Strictly *entre nous*,' Lomax quietly urged. 'Whatever passes between you and me – in one ear and out t'other. My word on it.'

Lomax was of the old school that still believed its word to be the golden key; and, as far as Coast was aware, Lomax's word was exactly that. And when he looked at Lomax, at the perceptive eyes, the frowned anxiety, the stilled hands cupped about a cigarette, he realised that the Section's buffoon was not drunk and not maudlin, but aware, and sharp, and that some significant change had occurred and that Lomax had observed it, whatever it was. And that he, Coast, did not know about it.

'Give me a for instance,' he said.

'Quilter's out today; right?' Lomax said, after a moment.

'And I haven't received a single communication from anywhere. But tomorrow, he'll be back. And tomorrow morning, when Goldie brings the mail around, I shall doubtless receive a letter or two, and a telex or two, with today's date on them. And this morning, when I used the Xerox machine, Heatherington wasn't in the Registry; but then he came back, just as I was going out – and I'd left the master I'd been copying on the machine – and when I went back for it, Heatherington had got the plate off the side of the machine and was checking the bloody counter – to see exactly how many copies I'd made. I tell you, old boy, it smells. I'm being watched. I've been in the Firm a long time. I've been a watcher myself, know all the ropes.'

'Heatherington watches everybody. It's part of his job.'

But Lomax would not be sidetracked. His plump hands circled his glass, but still did not pick it up.

'Quilter was out on Monday morning, too,' he said. 'Until half-past ten; and the mail I usually get at nine-thirty floated on to my desk at eleven fifteen.'

'Opened?'

'Not obviously; no,' admitted Lomax. 'But grubby around the edges. As if it had been.'

His case made, Lomax at last sat upright and picked up his drink.

' – And you don't know?' he said.

'No,' Coast replied frankly. 'I don't.'

Lomax stubbed out his cigarette and rubbed cigarette-ash from his thumb and forefinger over the ashtray.

'Look, old boy,' he said. 'I've half a mind to collar Quilter myself and ask him straight out. – Except that the other half reckons you could get it out of him better.' One corner of his mouth rose as he struggled for a touch of humour. 'After all, not a sparrow falls, as the Good Book says, unless the Deputy Head of Section wots of it. Isn't that right?'

'I'll have a word with Quilter,' Coast said.

Lomax's huge frame subsided with relief like a deflating party-balloon.

'Thanks, old boy,' he said. 'Knew you could be relied upon. Fancy another?'

All that afternoon, and on Thursday, Quilter was singularly elusive and came and went with great dispatch; and not until Friday morning, quite late on, did Coast finally succeed in waylaying him in his office. With a duster in his hand, Quilter was cleaning the leaves of his rubber-plant.

He smiled guiltily. 'Part of a meditative process, Jocelyn. – Do come in.'

Coast shut the door; it had been open and held back by a rubber wedge to let the breeze through. Quilter's ashtray was littered with cigarette ends.

Quilter folded the duster neatly and dropped it into the bottom drawer of his desk.

'What can I do for you?'

'I don't know, Tony,' said Coast, sitting down opposite him. Quilter's desk was unusually empty. 'Except that it's about Lomax.'

Quilter's face became instantly devoid of expression. He steepled his fingertips under his chin.

'And what about Lomax?' he said.

'Some cock and bull story about his mail being intercepted.'

Quilter didn't at once reply. His batrachian gaze remained unwavering.

'I told him he was imagining it.'

'He isn't,' said Quilter, abruptly. 'I only wish to hell he was.'

Coast scowled.

'You might have advised me,' he said.

Big Ben struck noon. A long silence followed. One of Quilter's hands reached out, crablike, for a shorthand notebook on his blotter and drew it fractionally closer to him. It was an unnecessary gesture, a purchase of time while he worked on making a decision of some sort.

'Yes, Jocelyn,' he said, at last. 'It was remiss of me. I should have done. I'm sorry.'

'You've put me in a spot, Tony. You realise that, don't you?'

Quilter regarded him levelly.

'What are you doing for lunch?' he said.

It was at that lunch that Quilter dropped his bombshell. His club went in for cramped little eating-rooms, panelled cubicles with a faded elegance, rather like the *salles priveés* of an Edwardian whorehouse that has fallen on hard times.

'We have a leak, Jocelyn.'

And when Quilter had said that the cubicle seemed to tilt. Quilter's head had been down as he sprinkled salt over his underdone roast potatoes, and he had glanced up again while Coast had still been trying to adjust his expression. 'One of us, Jocelyn. Any ideas?'

That had been the bombshell; but between the sprinkling and the upward glance, Coast had managed to stifle most of the skitterings of fear, the mask needed only the slightest extra adjustment to make it register blank surprise.

'You can't be serious, surely?'

'Deadly and pressingly,' Quilter replied, applying himself now to the pepper shaker.

There was evidence enough to indicate that this was no flash in the pan leak, no passing touch of nocturnal incontinence. It had been going on for ten years, possibly as far back as Foster's time.

'And how hard is it, Tony. This evidence.'

'Word of mouth. – But from Washington. Convincing enough, believe me.'

'And to Washington by way of whom?'

'Someone in 2D,' replied Quilter. 'Someone in Dzerzhinski Square.'

Coast contrived a laugh with a hook on it, a baited question mark that he left to float around the parchment lampshade.

'Oh, surely ... ' Pie in the sky stuff, the laugh said. Not us. Not E12.

But it was surely. A senior man – somebody in the upper echelons of the Second Directorate of the KGB – was wooing

Washington; and to make plain his seniority he was feeding back East-going Western intelligence of a remarkably high order. As yet he had no name. Only a code. To the CIA, as yet, he was only Minaret.

Coast ventured cautiously, 'Then he's obviously in a position to name names, by the sound of it? Has he? Yet?'

' – He can't. He won't. If he did that, he would blow himself, you see.' Quilter the ex-schoolmaster was still occasionally didactic. For a couple of years after Oxford he had taught political science at an obscure public school with spartan overtones in north Yorkshire.

And the conversation that had begun with reference to Eric Lomax now became a guessing game.

Could it be Toler?

Could it be Wesley?

Franklin? Heatherington, who guarded the Registry and the strong-room?

Names proposed, names dismissed. Those dismissed were men whose time in the Section was too short. Few went back as far as Foster. Others did not have access to certain areas of information – the Section had always been assembled from half a dozen watertight little boxes, left and right hands working separately from isolated halves of independent brains. Only at the top did teamwork start, were the threads finally drawn together and woven into the warp. There were certain eyes for this, and certain eyes for that. And the man in question had to be a time server, middle-aged, one of the trusties, someone with access to the Registry and keys to the strong-room – even Heatherington did not go in there on his own.

'Have you thought of me, Tony?'

Quilter's eyebrows shot up in mock horror at this bad joke.

'Morris?'

But the name to say, the one Quilter wanted to hear, was that of Eric Lomax. Coast could almost see him savouring it, rolling it around his tongue like a rare wine.

' – Lomax.'

And again, Coast managed to leave the question-mark in suspension and make Lomax sound like a slip of the tongue, a shot so wide of the mark that it had to be pursued and caught up again, before it had even struck the ground.

'You know something that I don't?' asked Quilter, not entirely certain whether he had seen the curve of the shot or not; or so he made it seem.

The glimmer of fear had slipped back below the horizon. Quilter's face was so easy to read. There was no hard evidence, only suspicion, a few randomly sown seeds, not heeled in and watered yet.

'No, not at all. I've run out of names, Tony. Forget it.'

But Quilter would not forget it.

'But something in the way you said it. It sounded considered ... '

' ... Well, I'm sure I didn't intend it to be ... '

'I want him watched,' said Quilter, suddenly the Head of Section, brooking no argument.

Coast still felt a nervous edge. Had it not been for that, this conversation would have held an element of farce. Lomax was the bumbler, at least on the surface. He was too clumsy for the quick pass, the furtive hand-over in the back of a taxi, the purposeful zigzags and backtracking on the way to a meet, the slyness.

'Oh, come on, Tony, you can't possibly be serious. Eric Lomax? A bloody traitor?'

'I haven't used the word,' Quilter said, evasively, prodding up peas. 'And of course I can't even be remotely sure that Lomax *is* involved.'

'But you'd like him to be.'

Quilter scowled.

'What a monstrous accusation, Jocelyn. *Like?* You make it sound as if I've drawn his name out of a hat, and am trying to make it fit a set of circumstances.'

'But you have a gut-feeling? Look, I know he drinks too much, Tony, but he's only got another year to go ... '

'I'm not looking for a scapegoat,' Quilter interrupted

brusquely. 'We're all under suspicion. It merely struck me that Lomax is the only one left of the old brigade of Foster's who hasn't stayed in step with the rest of us. It's as if he chooses deliberately to be a boozy grotesque – when the one thing I know he isn't, is a buffoon.'

'I tell you one thing, Tony, he's not so boozy that he hasn't noticed Heatherington keeping a special eye on him.'

Quilter did not miss the implication.

'I've given Heatherington instructions to clamp down on everyone,' he said. 'I certainly haven't asked him to single Lomax out.'

'Then you've overcooked it, Tony. He suspects you're gunning for him and I don't think that's altogether wise at this juncture, do you?'

Quilter grudgingly conceded that he might have acted more in haste than considered judgement, but only grudgingly. In the meantime, Lomax was to be closely monitored.

'Perhaps you might, Jocelyn,' Quilter had proposed hesitantly. 'I know that the two of you are old colleagues. – But you would have the time to do it more discreetly perhaps ... '

*

On Friday evening Lomax was waiting for him in the crowded buffet in Victoria Station. He had annexed a table in the corner and kept a seat vacant for Coast by the crude expedient of putting his bowler, briefcase and umbrella on it. He gathered them all over to his own side as Coast pushed his way through a gaggle of French students and joined him. A double Scotch was set up beside an as yet untouched vodka, and Lomax's evening paper was soggy in one corner from a puddle of beer.

'Cheers, old boy.'

'Good luck.'

It wasn't the evening for whisky and the jammed buffet was a cross between a baker's oven and a steam bath. And since lunchtime the world had taken on a new and disquieting perspective.

'How did it go, old boy?'

The whisky burned, and tasted acrid.

'About that, mostly.' Coast made a quick dip of his head towards the glass in Lomax's hand; although Quilter had mentioned Lomax's drinking only in passing. The Section had a leak and that leak was very likely Eric Lomax. That was what Quilter had hinted at. Mostly.

' – And I didn't exactly get the impression that there were any knives out.'

Lomax was not entirely convinced.

'Wouldn't have me on, would you, old boy?'

'It wouldn't be in my interests, Eric. Just lay off that stuff.'

'Hard, old boy. Not even sure I can.'

'Well, you'd better bloody try.'

When they came from the buffet and made their way to the ticket-barrier, Lomax was continuing the story he had begun over his third vodka.

' – Anyway to put the lid on it, one of these dam' terrorists came back last night and questioned both of us – you know the way they do it: moving around, picking up things and looking underneath and asking questions over their shoulders ... '

The story was a complicated one, something about Lomax's wife parking the car in Redhill yesterday while she did some shopping, then coming back and finding the car, with a new dent in the front wing, in a different place in the car park. When she arrived home there was a CID man waiting on the front doorstep. The car had been concerned in an accident. Personal injury was involved. A criminal offence, since Katerina had not reported the accident. Another detective had come back last night while Lomax was eating his dinner and questioned Kat again for an hour or more. But this morning, early, there had been a telephone call from the first detective. It was the right make and colour of car, but the wrong registration-number. Another eye-witness had come forward and the right culprit apprehended.

' – Very apologetic. But I tell you, old boy, this country isn't what it was.'

Lomax was either stupid or an innocent. His rambling story sounded more like a Special Branch scenario to get into his house and size it up without a warrant. He was clearly more under suspicion than Quilter had let on.

Quilter would have to be tackled again on Monday; first thing.

Five

At eight o'clock on that same evening, Coast was riffling through the paperbacks displayed on the carousel in the reception lobby of the Royal Lancaster Hotel.

After lunch, on the pretext that he had run out of cigarettes, Coast had parted from Quilter at Admiralty Arch and immediately walked along the Strand as far as Charing Cross station. And in the appointed telephone booth he had rung the number in Battersea and asked to speak to Michael. To make telephone contact was a clumsy business. Whoever was at Battersea had to go out to the nearest public call-box and dial back to the booth at Charing Cross station. They had taken a long time today, all of ten minutes, while he stood in the booth with the receiver to his ear and his fingers holding down the rest, ready to snatch them off again at the first tinkle of the bell. Today, a queue had formed behind him and two policemen in conversation had stood close enough to where he was for him to be able to read the silver insignia on the epaulettes of their shirts.

The voice had been a woman's.

'You aren't Michael. I wanted to speak to Michael.'

'Michael is out. You can speak to me.'

He had kept his self-control with difficulty. He took all the risks. They took none. At the first whiff of trouble they could take the next Aeroflot back to Mother Russia.

'I'm sorry,' he said. 'I only deal with Michael.'

And then he had put the phone down.

For diplomatic reasons, so Quilter had said, a temporary burst of opportunist passion between Washington and

Moscow, the defector's crossing was several weeks away. August at the earliest. And not a word, Jocelyn. This is strictly privy. Even if Mingay broaches the subject to you, you know nothing of it. Remember that.

He had spun out the afternoon being coldly rational, but since Lomax's story about the car it was plain that Lomax was being made the subject of a thorough investigation. And that had made him edgy again. He had to make plans of his own, buy time, make contact with Michael.

But then, glancing up, he saw Roma Peterson crossing the lobby. She was clad in unrelieved black, apart from a scarlet evening-shawl over her arm, and wore a smile for him that spoke already of old conspiracies. At ten yards, short and dark and tightly harnessed into all the right curves, she looked as glossy as an expensive china doll fresh from its box and swathes of tissue-paper.

Only close up did she disappoint. At a yard, she looked the thirty-seven or eight she was and her perfume was too cloyingly sweet, but what she leaned against him when she offered her cheek was tantalisingly and amorously female had he been in the mood for it.

'Lovely,' he said, cupping her elbows and letting his eyes rove hungrily over her face, a lover's trick that he had learned as a youth and over the years polished into an art-form. 'You look marvellous, splendid. How are you?'

'Oh, marvellous, splendid,' she mocked, smiling up at him with bright eyes, ravished already by all his signals, the tip of her tongue lurking behind her teeth like a moist, pink predator. 'You've obviously missed me.'

'Dam' right,' he said, and loosing one elbow he kept a proprietorial hold on the other as he steered her across the carpeted lobby. Between her two plump breasts depended the Egyptian *ankh* he had bought for her in Paris when he was still trying to get her into bed. Only belatedly had he discovered that he could have got her into it for nothing.

Out on the forecourt a pound note conjured up an instant taxi, and she sat close to him in the shadowy back of it, and let him feel the reassuring pressure of a glossy black leg and an affectionately warm thigh.

'Where are we going?'

'Somewhere private.'

The moist pink tongue flickered again behind her beautifully capped teeth.

'Where then?'

'Somewhere even more private.' And his reward was another of those soft throaty laughs that was perfectly aimed and wickedly effective. And close like this, feeling her heat, her womanly smells, in the pearly light of gathering dusk with the street lights just coming on, he was almost able to believe that this amorous camaraderie was something else, something worth fostering; except that the chill thinking part of him knew that it was not. But for a few hours, more if he was lucky, he was going to cast adrift Quilter, and Michael, and wayward defectors, and the occasional niggles of fear, and the spectral hand that was ever about to clamp hard upon his shoulder from behind, and just concentrate on this warm sensation that kept stealing about his groin; this knife-edge of a game that could only be played with a woman.

The somewhere private was in Highgate, very discreet, very French and very expensive. They dined at the rear of it, in what had once been an orangery, a Victorian confection of glass and lacey white ironwork, that looked as if it might have been pupped at Kew. The tables were spread well apart, and further isolated from each other by trellis screens interwoven with flowering clematis.

The soft glow of the Tiffany-shaded table lamps improved her, as had the tournedos Rossini and the bombe glacée and the Armagnac, and his frequent appreciative glances down the front of her dress. His ordering of the Nuits St. George had been a master stroke.

'You remembered,' she said; and he had, but only after he had scanned the wine list, not before.

Replete, and slightly drunk, she had now reached the stage of sleepy-eyed dalliance.

'What's Gus doing with himself these days?'

'Still hawking his lumber.' Peterson's Paris cover was a timber importing business in the northern suburbs. 'Like you do.' She sipped at her second Armagnac, and smiled across at him with a lopsided shrewdness. ' – Or do you?'

'Do I what?'

'Sell lumber.' Her eyes fixed him, slightly out of focus, already half in the bedroom. 'I don't think you do. Not really.'

A small thrill of alarm. He smiled back, carefully adjusting the expression to lie somewhere between hidden mystery and amicable randiness.

'Why on earth should you think that?'

'You're too smart,' she said. 'Too smoothly lascivious. Banking I'd believe. But not lumber. I bet you couldn't name me half a dozen usable trees.'

'Try me.'

One of her legs flirted between his own under the table. 'It's late,' she said. 'And I can think of better things to talk about.'

She knew nothing. She was drunk. It was only talking for talking's sake. The desire he had felt for her in the taxi was gone long since. His isolation from the rest of humankind was still not an habitual way of life, and he ached sometimes for the sort of woman that Frances had been, intelligent, sexy, easy to be with.

Patiently he steered her back on to conversational course.

She was in London for ten days on a shopping spree. She had wheedled five thousand dollars-worth of American Express travellers' cheques out of Gus: she wasn't sure, but she thought that he had just signed a big deal of some sort.

' – And I told him I refused to stay in Paris on my own.'

'You mean he's gone somewhere?'

She shrugged dispassionately.

'Hamburg. Somewhere like that. He never says. I have to pick up whatever I can on the bedroom extension.'

His ears pricked. For whatever reason Peterson had gone to Hamburg, it was very unlikely to be to oversee a consignment of timber at the docks.

'Lubeck,' she said. 'I just remembered.'

'I'm sorry ... ?'

'Lubeck,' she said. 'Hamburg – then he's going on to Lubeck.'

'Till when?'

'Oh, hell,' she said, flapping away Peterson on an airy gesture. 'Who cares.'

He decided that would be a task for later, when she was nearer sober, to beguile from her in the cosy few minutes of post-coital aftermath over a shared cigarette. Peterson worked on the Paris embassies circuit, and Lubeck was up on the Baltic coast of West Germany, and within spitting distance of the German Democratic Republic. Cross one field too many and you could defect by accident.

In the dark back of the taxi her red bud of a doll's mouth opened wide enough to devour him. The inside of it was fiery with Armagnac, luxurious and aphrodisial, and what he had begun in cold blood again became a need, for comfort, for fleshly warmth, almost for love. Loneliness had too many allies working for it; he had none.

'It's right, that old cliché,' she whispered on a choked breath.

'Which one?'

'The one about absence ... you know?' Then the doll's mouth opened wide again.

On the way up to his flat, in the lift, she kept a tight grip on him, and the talk was of the days in Paris, tonight, tomorrow, next week; perhaps she could persuade Gus to send some more traveller's cheques. Her eyes had taken on the glazed heavy-liddedness of the drug-addict and her body was slumped heavily against him, belly to belly, and there were no Quilters or Michaels or spectral hands anywhere in sight.

In the flat she followed him about like a curious puppy while he got a tray of ice out of the refrigerator and poured them each a drink.

'I thought you'd live smarter than this,' she said, her vacuous eyes looking all about.

'No need,' he said. 'I'm hardly ever here.'

'Where are you then? – Some woman, I'll bet.'

'I should be so lucky,' he said, and she laughed and slopped her drink all over her dress as she fastened on to him again. He steered her into the bedroom, and by the light spilling in from the lobby he unzipped her and shucked her out of the black dress. She took off the rest herself and waited for him on the bed, squirming against him the moment he touched her.

'You need a bigger bed,' she said. 'I like to manoeuvre.'

He made a laughing sound, his face blank in the shelter of the dark as he settled over her. Her climax came quickly, her body going tight like a bowstring, and then was abandoned like a stricken vessel, but for him, for a long time, there was nothing. In Paris, it had been curiosity that had drawn him to her, her vivacious sexiness, the promise of all those tight little curves, the thrill of the chase, the touch of risk that was always there with another man's wife.

And again her soft squeal of delight broke at his ear, but still there was nothing for him; until he thought of Frances, the girl-Frances, Frances hot and damp and naked against the bathroom wall until she sagged against him in joyous release; and afterwards they had gone along to the Lomax's and she had looked as if butter wouldn't melt in her mouth.

Or Frances after an evening out somewhere, an evening that had been special; her evening dress hung over the back of a chair, standing in front of the dressing mirror, in her stockings and high heels and bra and a pair of miniscule briefs that only enhanced her gender and disguised nothing while she pretended to brush her hair, because the evening *had* been special and because she knew that to see her like that turned him on like nothing else ever did. And while he had been in the bathroom, the packet of contraceptives and a stack of paper handkerchiefs had already been disposed on the cabinet beside the bed.

And they'd played the goat a little, first.

He used to leer and crook a finger.

'Hey,' he'd say. 'You. *Viens.*'

And over she'd come with a bit of a wiggle, a strip-teaser's walk, with a sussuration of nylon, and he would feel the cold back of her hairbrush against the nape of his neck.

'*Quoi?*' she used to ask, smiling up at him.

'You know bloody well *quoi*,' he'd say, then growl at her and nip at her upturned chin. 'You've got legs like a bloody Lido-girl: know that?' And as he gasped his own pinchbeck raptures into mouthfuls of black hair, Roma Peterson thought it was all for her and her body rippled and all the wounded-animal sounds came out of it again.

For a long time afterwards he couldn't draw breath, stifled with hair and pillow and the greedy body that still pecked avidly at his uselessness. And slumped there, he knew that one day he would go like this, stone cold in the arms of some terrified woman he scarcely knew, jerking his way to oblivion, and at last finding it. While Roma Peterson sprawled beneath him in plump contentment because she, unlike him, really had mistaken this fleeting satiation for something else, the oldest illusion.

The cigarette passed from hand to hand. The ball of orange light from it glowed then diminished again. With a hand curled possessively over his leg she was still pouring out her inanities. That magic, that something that made two people click together they way they did. Gus was impotent. Either that, or he had another woman somewhere; not that she cared.

In the occasional orange glow, the breasts that had been hampered together as tightly as a pair of adolescent buttocks now sagged distastefully and there was a black-shadowed crease across her abdomen.

'Perhaps he's got a woman in Lubeck.'

'No,' she said. 'It's business. I heard him on the phone. – He's been like a dog with two tails for days. I think he's been promoted.'

'To what?'

She didn't know. Except that it was to do with transport. He'd got all these maps about the apartment. He was marking them all up with felt-tipped pens.

'Maps of where?'

Her little finger began to stroke at him. Gus was already a bore, and the cigarette went into the ashtray.

When he woke in the loneliest hours, the first thing to leap into his mind was the lunchtime revelation of Quilter's; the next was the story Lomax had told about Katerina and the car. The dogs were sniffing. The trail would have to dry up for a little while; he'd have to make that clear to Michael. What he would also have to do was to play up to Quilter about Lomax. Of course, they'd find out in time that it wasn't Lomax, that the old buffoon was simply a middle-class Civil Servant whose only ambition was to drink away his pension when the time was ripe. But perhaps by the time they had found that out, Michael would have got word back to Moscow, and Minaret would be arrested where he sat at his desk in Dzerzhinski Square; the matter might then die. Even the Foster business had never really come to anything in the end. His thinking was jumbled, one ramshackle thought following another. What terrified him most was his sensation of insularity. He hadn't even got a regular woman any more. He had faced forty with comparative indifference. Fifty, he feared. Fifty was the major turning point, possibly even the finishing line.

When he reached for Roma Peterson she shifted irritably. She murmured drowsily, 'Lay off, Gus, for Christ's sakes,' and pushed out at him and rolled away.

But in the morning she was skittishly affectionate, parading about in her tights and her underwear while she painted her face. And for him nothing stirred. In the chill light of another Saturday she was even closer to forty than she had been last night. The flesh of her waist and arms was already beginning to slacken and an army of fatty dimples were marching relentlessly up her thighs and across her buttocks. It took a conscious effort to mask his distaste and play along with her; because now he definitely had to play along with her.

She had given him Peterson's letter in much the same way as she would have rewarded a pet poodle with a particularly succulent bone. It had been an afterthought. She had come upon it while she had been rummaging about in her handbag for her lipstick.

'I haven't the faintest idea what's in it.' The lipstick momentarily stopped in mid-stroke and she smiled archly at him through the mirror. 'Not having an affair, you two, are you?'

She was free all day – and tomorrow.

'I'm sorry, Roma,' he said. 'I'm seeing my daughter today.'

'I didn't know you had one.'

She turned her back to be zipped. Tightly cased she was almost desirable again, but he would not succumb, not until absolutely necessary.

'What's her name?'

'Susan.'

'How old is she?'

'Fourteen.'

She turned and leaned against him, the subject of Susan already forgotten, sliding her arms about his waist.

'Marvellous; last night. Even better than Paris.'

Somehow he found more appropriate words, but even against the heat of her stomach and the feel of her buttocks under the slippery black dress still nothing stirred in him.

'When do I see you again?'

He smiled down at her. A foot away, in daylight, her eyes were quite dull and bovine. Last night she had been able to tell him nothing because she knew nothing. And all he presently wanted to do was to rip open the envelope that with studied casualness he had tucked into his wallet, where it was now burning a hole.

'Soon,' he said.

She made a little moué. At eighteen she could have got away with it; twenty years on she could not.

'Too vague,' she said.

'Tomorrow,' he said. And tomorrow it would be Monday and on Monday, Tuesday. 'Definitely.'

He drove her back through the Saturday morning traffic to the Royal Lancaster. It took the best part of an hour, while she talked incessantly, sure that she possessed him.

The forecourt was lined with taxis, taking on and putting down, ranks of suitcases.

'Stay for lunch.' The red bud hovered temptingly a couple of inches below his chin as he leaned across to open the door for her.

'Sorry. Late already.' He brushed the bud, and still nothing stirred, although he had to pretend otherwise. He moved forward a couple of yards as a taxi-horn blasted impatiently close behind and gave him the parting excuse he needed. 'I'll give you a ring. – Tuesday at the latest.'

'Don't forget.'

'I shan't.'

He watched her go in, full of aplomb, her behind swaying under the skimpy black dress, saw the commissionaire hold the door for her. She raised a hand. He waved back with clinical detachment.

He ripped open the letter in the first back street where there was a space to park.

Peterson still believed in the anonymity of the typewriter. There were two pages of it, but one word leapt out at him at the first scan. It was the word Quilter had spoken at Friday lunchtime. Minaret. Peterson was suggesting a meet.

The spectre was gaining substance.

He drove straightway to Charing Cross station. Again it was the woman who answered; but this time he could not afford to play the prima donna.

'I want a meet,' he said. 'It's important.'

'Monday,' she said. 'The Hampstead house. I will arrange it.'

'Not sooner?'

'Michael is away for the weekend. I cannot contact him.'

He reluctantly settled for that. He felt better after he had made the call. Michael, whoever the current one was, would know what to do.

He spent the rest of the weekend making mental

short-lists, but the possibilities were few. Morris, Toler and Franklin were hard-line Right-wingers, Queen and Country, with County wives and too much to lose. Wesley was too new to the Section, so was Heatherington, so was the Goldring woman. Templeton was likely, paying alimony to two wives and with the third already on the horizon; he had a small private income, but not half enough. Fanning, too, was a remote possibility; he had also once been frowned upon: a son given a suspended sentence for drug possession, a daughter who had been twice arrested in Grosvenor Square in the riotous days of the late 'sixties.

But the one name that kept returning inescapably to head the list was that of Eric Lomax, the most unlikely of all of them. God alone knew what had put it into Quilter's head. Mere dislike, perhaps; or even a kind of jealousy harboured somewhere in Quilter's small mind. Quilter was only an ex-schoolmaster, an academic with a flair for organisation and a patience with petty paperwork. Unlike Lomax, and Morris and Toler and Franklin and Fanning and Templeton, and Coast himself, Quilter had never been out into the field, and his only stint outside Whitehall had been a six-month tour in Washington as an ad hoc junior member of the embassy staff.

Of the real nuts and bolts Quilter knew nothing. If he had, he would have seen how unsuitable Lomax was for the role in which he had cast him. A working traitor was the last link in a tenuous chain that led back to Moscow or East Berlin or Warsaw or Prague; and this end of the chain was staked down in the enemy camp, where one could only traffick under license and tread with caution, and only get drunk alone and out of sight.

Peterson's letter need not pass under Quilter's nose for a week – or even at all. There was no reason why it should. So far as he was aware, all assignations were going to be posted in the Daily Telegraph. Quilter would never know under what circumstances, or when, he had come into possession even if he did have to show it to him. And a week would give the people at Battersea a fair chance of getting what was known so far back to Moscow in the diplomatic bag. They might be able to nail Minaret before he did any more damage.

The first hour of Monday was invariably dedicated to chaos, this morning more than usually so. Wesley was on leave, Fanning had not turned in, and Goldring had still not typed the four-line memo he had dictated to her on Friday afternoon.
'Why not?'
Her eyes struck out at him like cold knives.
'Because I'm setting up a report on the processor for Mr. Quilter.'
'You've got a typewriter, haven't you?'
'I've only got one pair of hands, Mr. Coast. If you've got any complaints, I suggest you have a word with Mr. Quilter.'
It was a bad start, even for a Monday, and there was also the inevitable moment or two of chimerical thoughts. An East-to-West defection was always a dangerous event, the defector put on public display only when he had dropped the names of the guilty in private. For weeks afterwards the unnamed guilty had to walk a tightrope.

Six

He had taken a circuitous route to Hampstead by bus and Tube, jumping from both only as the doors were closing.

He entered the tall block of flats in the gathering dusk. A zealous estate-agent would have described it as a mansion-block, and with justification. It overlooked the Heath and at least two cabinet-ministers and the mistress of another were resident in it. The entrance hall was empty. He took the lift to the fifth floor, then walked down to the third, then stood for at least a minute looking down the stair-well and listening. There were no dogging footsteps.

Apart from the two brass numbers screwed to it, there was nothing to distinguish Number 26 from any of the other mahogany-faced doors. He rapped lightly with his knuckles, and as the door opened he stepped forward and in with one last backward glance along the passage.

The door was closed, the lobby absorbing him into its darkness until a switch clicked and the light came on.

The new Michael was a small dark man with pale wet eyes. He wore a baggy blue suit with a bright white pinstripe, a blood-red handkerchief drooping like a limp tongue from his breast pocket. Nearly seventy years after their revolution they still hadn't learned to cut a decent suit or knew how to dress.

They exchanged trading-names. Anthony. Michael. Suspicion hung between them like a grey cloud.

'You are very late.'

'Trouble on the Tube. I'm sorry.'

The other turned away pettishly and Coast followed him

into a long lounge, where the furniture was corpsed under white dust sheets and a pair of painters' steps with a boiler-suit slung over them stood astride by the window. The place reeked of new paint.

The little man went to an attaché case lying on one of the shrouded armchairs and took out a hip-flask and two cheap drinking glasses. Without asking, he half filled both with whisky and held one out.

'I take it you were not followed.'

'Silly question. I won't even bother to answer it.'

The moist grey eyes flickered briefly to life as Coast took one of the proffered glasses.

'That sort of thing is important. – And we are both on the same side.'

'You people come and go,' Coast retorted. 'People like me have to live with it all the time.'

Michael indicated a chair. Most of his lack of stature lay in his legs, and when he straddled the covered arm of the settee only his toes touched the carpet. The early Michaels had been diplomats, men of education. Their quality had diminished.

'The people at the Centre were pleased with your last consignment,' he said. 'A successful approach has already been made to a Colonel in the Netherlands Air Force.' The wet eyes floated above a patronising smile. 'So, you see, the net widens.'

The lights were coming on across the far side of the Heath. The uncurtained windows lent the lit room an unpleasant ambience of vulnerability.

'Don't crow too soon. The traffic flows both ways. There's a defection coming up, one of our people.'

The moist eyes came to life again.

'How do you know?'

Coast brought out Peterson's letter from his wallet.

'From whom?' asked Michael, leaning forward to reach for it.

'A CIA operator. Privately.'

Michael read it with laboured care, his face immobile.

'This is not proof. It is only pieces of paper. It could have been typed by anyone.'

'The name of Minaret was given to me hours before I saw that letter. Whoever Minaret is, he or she is in our pipeline. That makes both of us an interested party.'

Michael started to put the letter in his pocket. Coast clicked his fingers.

'Sorry,' he said. 'The only way you pass that on is a copy in your own handwriting.'

Michael reluctantly handed the letter back.

'You do not trust me?'

'This isn't a sentimental business,' Coast reminded him. ' – If this letter goes to Moscow it will have to be watched all the way. Step by step. If it isn't, I stand to be crucified.'

Michael hitched one shoulder.

'One telephone call, and we would have you out of this country within hours. We always look after our own people.'

'So I'm told.'

'It is true. There has not been a major spy trial in your country for twenty years. You should stop and ask yourself why.'

He drained his glass, filled it again, then offered Coast the leather-bound flask.

Coast declined. The journey back to Streatham Hill would be equally circuitous.

'Please. I shall make a copy.'

Coast passed the letter back. Michael went down on the settee with his attaché case on his knees and took a shorthand notebook from it. He wrote as he read, letter by laborious letter, occasionally lapsing into Cyrillic where a phrase was instantly translatable.

In the old days of Michael One, when the meetings had been regular, Coast had been able to drop his guard but the habit had been lost. No longer was it possible to use the meet like a confessional the way it used to be, the ritual letting down of hair, the amicable dialogues. The first Michael had been a family man; this seedy-looking lay-brother from a trade mission was a man alone.

With its view across the Heath the flat was obviously an expensive one, and he wondered who the owner was. The chandelier looked like an adapted antique and the brass and glass coffee table had never come off a production line in Taiwan. Beyond the windows night had overtaken dusk.

Michael's ballpoint pen stopped, was capped, and he passed back Peterson's letter.

'Does anyone know you have that?'

'No one.'

'And you think that Minaret is in the chain – somewhere?'

'Not think. I know he is.'

He repeated the substance of Friday's conversation in Quilter's club. Michael made no notes, but sat with his head tilted forward and slightly to one side with a quiet alertness. His hair was long, and slicked down with too much brilliantine, and at the nape of his neck it curled upward over his white shirt collar. He was certainly not a Slav. His eyes had a distinct slant at their outer corners; probably a Georgian.

'This meeting with your CIA man,' he said, tapping his pad with the cap end of the ballpoint pen. 'Can you go?'

'Risky.'

'It always is.'

Coast smiled grimly.

'I meant more of a risk than usual.'

'You made the choice in the first place yourself,' Michael reminded him. 'You were not coerced.' The moist eyes narrowed against Coast's chill look of response, and hostility surfaced again in the silence. Coast suppressed his by a conscious effort of will. There was no point in a slanging-match. This shabby looking little clerk-*nik* was probably programmed with dialectic like a computer.

'It's on Saturday,' said Coast. 'Short notice. And we're right in the middle of the tourist season. It could be difficult to book a flight.'

'There is nothing that cannot be arranged. You could take the early flight on Saturday, meet this Peterson on Saturday afternoon; and catch an early evening flight back. No one need ever know you have been away.'

'Except for the stamps in my passport.'

'We gave you another. To all intents and purposes it is genuine.'

The other passport was his escape passport. The one he would have to use if things ever got too tight. The one they would spirit him away with.

'And what happens when I really need it?'

Michael hunched his shoulders and let them fall again.

'We shall arrange for another. It is a simple matter. Trust me.'

'I shall need money. Expenses.'

Clamping his notebook to the lid with the flat of his hand, Michael opened his attaché case far enough to slide a hand in up to the wrist. The hand came out clutching a thick wad of mixed denomination bank-notes held together with a red elastic band. He licked a finger and counted out ten five pound notes and twenty tens.

'That should be enough,' he said, stretching forward to hand them over. 'And do not worry. They are old – and well-laundered, as they say. They are completely untraceable. Buy travellers' cheques. We will see to the tickets.'

'And how do I lay my hands on them?'

'The post. We shall post them to you.'

'Hardly secure.'

Michael smiled. 'In England, my friend, one can even send a bomb through the post with comparative security.'

Michael pondered, his thin lower lip rolled forward.

'And you think,' he said, 'That the CIA have only warned your people of the possibility of this defection? They have not passed on any details?'

'Hardly.'

'But Peterson knows?'

'So it seems.'

'So.' Michael put his case on the cushion beside him and leaned back in the settee. 'Assuming Peterson is part of this defection – and you are his only control – and assuming that that letter is not shown to your superiors – it is possible that you could look into this matter without your MI ever knowing about it.'

'I'd be putting myself on the line – especially if your people spike the operation.'

'It will be done with care. I promise you.' Michael smiled urbanely. 'We might even be able to substitute a Minaret we approve of. Think of that, my friend. Eh?' This fantasy seemed to please him and he spent a moment or two savouring it.

For a while then they drifted into more mundane matters, the washroom tittle-tattle, the raw meat of a few telexes, the imminent changes to the NATO cipher routines.

But, inevitably, the conversation reverted to Operation Minaret.

'Your contact, Peterson; perhaps he would also work for us.'

'Too complicated; and he isn't our sort of material.'

Michael did not press the point.

'I think,' he said. 'That your first objective is to concentrate on the Lomax diversion. If Quilter suspects that Lomax is the source of your leak, you must make sure that he continues to think so.'

'Easier said than done,' said Coast. That Lomax was a spy was farcical. And it wouldn't take long for the Special Branch to sort that out.

'Guy Burgess was also a buffoon,' Michael pointed out. He had that peculiar mid-transatlantic accent that so many Russians acquire through learning English by way of American gramophone records. 'He was also a drunkard; he was also a homosexual; he was also one of our best operators. So why not this man Lomax?'

'I'm still asking myself why Quilter selected him in the first place. He just isn't right.'

'That is not our problem,' said Michael, abruptly cutting Coast off with a sideways flap of his hand. 'It is for us a tool. We must use it. Consolidate this suspicion with a few pieces of evidence.'

'They would have to be manufactured.'

'So manufacture them.' Michael folded his arms and became implacable. 'Make them. There is no alternative.' He shrugged. 'None.'

A long silence followed. Each gazed at the other without wavering. There were no externals, simply the space between them.

'I'll do my best,' said Coast. 'But at the first sign of anything going wrong, I want out. Do you understand? A place to put my feet up, with no hassle.'

'A small price for what you have done for us,' said Michael. He had relaxed again, and his hands had fallen over his knees. 'And it has always been implicit in our arrangements.'

They shook hands behind the front door. Michael's was like a fistful of warm dry twigs.

'Stay calm,' he said. 'Keep in touch. Pass nothing. – And report to me here on Monday evening at the same time. Everything. Dates, times, places, whatever Peterson tells you.'

Prominently displayed on the lobby table, one corner weighted down by a glass ashtray, was a note from his cleaning woman to say that the electricity meter had been read that morning. He would have thought no more about it, had it not been for the two cups carelessly left on the kitchen draining-board. The meter reader had been invited to a cup of tea, and perhaps stayed for a chat.

Someone had been. Someone in authority, however petty that authority was.

Heatherington's desk was just inside the doorway of the Registry annexe. His closely cropped head was deedily bent over a set of index-cards he was making out, but at the sound of Coast's footsteps it lifted like a well-trained pointer. This was Heatherington's domain and his pale stare was as much a barrier as the waist-high hardboard fence and gate a few yards beyond his desk.

'Yessir?' he said, a parade-ground bark muted to a hoarse whisper, one felt, only by these claustrophobic circumstances into which his early retirement from the Coldstream Guards had led him.

'I want the green files for the last three months, Mr. Heatherington.'

'Sight or loan, sir?'

Coast smiled to cover his restlessness. 'Sight definitely; a loan perhaps.' It was Friday morning and still no opportunity had presented itself. With time slipping away, he was forced to make one.

Heatherington took his chain of keys from the top drawer of his desk and preceded Coast to the gate in the hardboard fence, his rubber soled shoes squeaking on the plastic tiles.

'Mrs. H. fit again?'

'Yessir. Thank you, sir. It was only a kidney-stone. Size of a peanut.'

'Good news all round, then.' Last week Heatherington had become a grandfather.

'Yessir.'

The door to the Registry stood open. Against the left hand wall squatted the Xerox machine and the automatic document-shredder. The files were stored on the right, in a floor to ceiling cage of wire-netting on wooden frames which took up three-quarters of the room and blocked out most of the light from the windows. Each aisle of metal shelving had its own wire-mesh gate and a separate light switch.

Heatherington sorted through his keys and unlocked the gate on the far right and reached inside for the switch.

'All yours, sir.'

'Thank you.'

The rubber soles squeaked away.

The green files were kept at the far end nearest the windows, but he did not go at once that far up the aisle. He could feel his heart flapping about and tasted the metallic flavour in his mouth. This was the first time he had ever attempted to take anything that had not passed through his hands by way of the normal office routines, and this was the first time that what he was doing had felt like wanton theft. Quickly, he bound a handkerchief about each hand as a makeshift glove and reached up for the first Adriatic file his eyes lit upon. He rifled through it as quietly as he could and as hastily as his eyes could scan the pages. Almost any sheet would have suited his purpose – but then he came upon a pink flimsy carbon copy – tabling the Greek Navy's Adriatic patrols and their radio-frequencies for the coming month of July – a quick manipulation of the fastening and the flimsy was out of the file. But then, for a second or two, paralysis overtook him as he heard Heatherington's chair scrape and his squeaky tread come back into the Registry.

And then the Xerox machine started up, and under cover of its noise he hurriedly folded the flimsy into four, then once again, and rammed it into his trouser pocket. Back with the file, off with the two handkerchiefs. The entire operation had taken a minute at most. It had seemed like an hour.

He went further up the aisle and took down an innocuous file of memoranda between himself and Quilter.

Heatherington and his penetrating stare were back on guard.

'Taking that one, are you, sir?'

The file was recorded in Heatherington's register, neatly in a block hand, the register turned, a red ball-point pen offered.

'Just there, sir, please.'

A spatulate finger-tip stood watch over the signature-box.

'Thank you.'

'Thank you, sir.'

'Back in an hour.'

'Long as you like, sir.'

He managed to regain his office before the shakes started. Using a handkerchief again, he slipped the folded pink sheet into his briefcase.

Lunchtime found him in a copy-bureau-cum-stationers in

Victoria Street, and he had to hang around for ten minutes or more before there was no one at all near the copier and the assistants were looking the other way. He used a handkerchief again to handle the sheets of paper, pretending to give his nose a couple of blows while the platten of the machine shunted forward and back, then quickly slid both the original and the copy into the open jaws of his briefcase.

At half past two he was back in the Registry.

'The wrong one, dam' it. I'm sorry.'

'That's all right, sir. No trouble.'

The file of memoranda was signed back.

'I'll put it back myself, Mr. Heatherington – and try to sort out the right one this time.'

'Much obliged, sir. Thank you.'

The ceremony of the keys and the light switch. Did fear have a smell, he wondered.

The file was returned, another equally innocuous one taken down. Putting back the flimsy, however, was more difficult than had been the taking out. Heatherington kept squeaking about outside on his Friday afternoon stint of tidying up and sealing the sacks of shredding-machine waste for the security van to take away; and the flimsy crackled noisily at its every unfolding. But efficient though Heatherington was, he was of the breed of man who could only do one thing at a time and his sealing machine clicked away steadily outside. The flimsy was laced back into place, the file slid endwise into its hanger.

'You'll bring that back by tonight, won't you, sir? With the week-end coming up. Mr. Quilter's got very hot about that just lately.'

'Yes, of course.'

The red pen, the spatulate finger-tip with its neatly manicured nail.

'Thank you, sir.' Heatherington glanced pointedly at the clock over the Registry door. 'Two hours, sir. Then I have to start locking-up.'

Back in his office, it was all of five minutes before he dared to take up a pen and put his signature to a couple of letters.

Seven

'Are you in the Federal Republic for business or pleasure, Herr Tavistock?'

'Business.'

The passport was stamped and slapped hard back into his hand.

At Customs he went through on the green, but was selected for a random check, although they didn't ask him to open his overnight bag.

'Nothing above the allotment of wines and cigarettes – no drugs – no medicinal substances?'

'No,' he said. 'Nothing at all.'

He caught the airport bus to the centre of the city. During the night Hamburg had suffered what looked like a flash storm and there were still deep lakes in some of the gutters where the drains had not been able to cope. Over on the right, stamped against a still featureless grey sky, Unilever Haus, with all its windows lit, seemed to tower above almost everything.

He lit a cigarette. His reflection in the bus window was that of a stranger. By simply parting his hair on the other side and putting on a pair of spectacles he had become John Gregory Tavistock. And to lend credence to his temporary persona, Mr. Tavistock carried in his wallet a plastic concertina of credit cards, a few visiting-cards, a couple of letters on the headed notepaper of his equally mythical employers, and even a photograph of a Mrs. Tavistock sitting in the Tavistock garden with the Tavistock West Highland terrier panting on her lap. Mr. Tavistock's

A Position of Trust

passport was a battered and, on the face of it, a much travelled document. It bore several small but quite important differences to Coast's own. According to Tavistock's passport, he was an inch shorter than Coast – few immigration officers carry tape measures – he had a small scar at the base of his right thumb – small enough for Coast's passport not to warrant declaring; and his eyes were grey rather than blue, because no one ever notices the colour of eyes unless they are spectacular in some way and belong to the opposite sex, and not always then. So Jocelyn Coast was John Tavistock, studiously bespectacled and shaggy of hair, with a wayward forelock of it hanging over his left eye. There was a look at once intellectual and vague about him, which was accidental – but suited the role of sales-director of an educational book publisher based in Hove. In the last hour and a half, Mr. Tavistock's entirely bogus passport had been subjected to three official scrutinies and survived all of them.

The cigarette lasted him as far as the Jungfernstieg where he and several other passengers debouched from the bus and went their separate ways. He stood for a few minutes watching the boats bobbing on Binnenalster, then walked smartly along the south-western edge of the lake until he came to a public toilet. He was in there for only a few minutes, and when he came out again he was Jocelyn Coast. He walked to the southwest then, mostly by way of the major streets and made his way to the St. Pauli landing-stage on the bank of the Elbe.

It was a long walk; but he had time to spare. It was still only eight-thirty and his meeting with Peterson was not until ten. He came to Hamburg rarely, and each time he came the city appeared to have sprouted more featureless towers of glass and concrete, clear proclamations that the new Hamburg was, like the old one, good for a thousand years; if it didn't get flattened again. More Turks about too, the new serfs, the *gastarbeiten* who swept the streets and portered at the stations, washed the dishes in the cafés and hotels. The men swarthy, the women wearing peasant's headscarves, still

Turks. From penury to slavery in one generation.

He bought himself a coffee and a rye roll in a café on the Reeperbahn. The amusement-arcades and strip-clubs were still being cleared of last night's débris and every few yards along the pavement edge stood a pile of black plastic refuse bags waiting for the city trash collectors to pick up. A few neon signs glowed with mournful indifference to the early hour.

At five to ten he was strolling down the Helgolander Allee towards the jetty where the water-buses tied up. The one Peterson would be on was still coming in, crabwise against the current, the municipal pennant fluttering at its masthead and its horn blaring at an errant yacht tacking across its bows. Its engine note went down a pitch as it reversed its propellers and slipped sideways towards the stage. Peterson was sitting on one of the bench seats near the wheel-house. He was dressed like a Sunday-morning Englishman this morning, tweed jacket, cavalry-twill trousers, a roll-neck brown pullover. A couple of hempen ropes were looped over bollards and the guard-chain taken off the boarding-ramp.

Peterson came up the slope briskly slapping a rolled up newspaper against his leg. As his wife had intimated, this was a newer and decidedly perkier Peterson than the one he had left in Paris, although he still, once or twice, cast a furtive glance about. But then he would probably do that on his deathbed.

His right hand was already out-thrust a half dozen paces away.

'Jocelyn, how are you?' he enquired, grinning, and pumping vigorously. 'How are you, old man.'

He was almost overwhelmingly excited. The newspaper continued to slap against his leg as he and Coast fell into step together. This was big, he confided. The biggest project he had ever tackled. It would retire him out of the Agency in a blaze of glory. This guy was no damned fag of a ballet-dancer, no two-bit revisionist poet from the Gulags hell-bent on collecting his American Royalties. He was a general. One-star, two-star, maybe even a three-star. They might know which across in Washington or Langley; but they were playing it that close to the chest that only two or three people perhaps knew how many pieces of metal were pinned to his shoulder-boards. But he had to be big. He even knew someone inside the Praesidium. There was no proof of that yet, but everything he had passed over so far was authentic, gilt-edged stock, and there was no reason to doubt that anything he said was equally authentic.

Peterson walked with spring in his stride. His face bore an expression akin to spiritual release. His centre of operations was up an alley off the Reeperbahn. An aluminium plaque on its door proclaimed it to be the Heider Escort Agency. The door had once been white, but now the paint was peeling to reveal a faded green beneath. Below the plaque, hand written on a piece of white card tucked into a plastic envelope and stapled to the door, another sign read that the Heider Agency was temporarily closed while Herr Heider took a holiday.

Peterson unlocked the door and led the way up a narrow but lushly carpeted flight of stairs. Its walls at each side were lined with framed photographs of the agency's stock-in-trade, white, black, oriental, and several shades between.

The door at the head of the stairs also carried an aluminium plaque similar to the one downstairs, and beside it was a chair for clients to sit on while they waited for audience of Herr Heider in his busier moments.

Peterson opened it up with a flourish, showed him in, then locked the door from the inside. The paper was tossed on to the desk that filled most of the pokey office. First things were always first with Peterson. A bottle of Teacher's was produced from the top drawer of the only filing cabinet and two glasses topped to the brim.

'Down the hatch,' he said. 'Well, what do you think?' He made a sweeping gesture to encompass the seedy confines of his operations-room.

The desk, the filing-cabinet and two chairs; and no telephone. There was a fire-escape outside the window, but the windows were steel-barred and only with a welding torch could egress be gained that way.

'Is it sterile?'

'Sure it's sterile.' Peterson sat down in the swivel-chair and opened a drawer in the desk. He brought out what looked like a pocket-sized transistor radio and displayed it on the blotter. 'It sweeps the VHF band from end to end,' he said. 'It'll pick up any bug inside a twenty foot radius. Believe me, this place is sterile.' The little box went back into the drawer, the drawer closed with a negligent push of his foot.

He lit a cigarette from the stub of the last one.

'So what do you want to know, Jocelyn?'

'Everything.'

Peterson's bonhomie temporarily fell away. His silver eyebrows fleeted momentarily together in a straight line.

'Like I said,' he said. 'It's all close to the chest.'

'Then I'll re-phrase it: everything *you* know.'

This was plainly Peterson's moment. He held the stage. He swung the chair back and forth; a few degrees this way, a few degrees the other way. He rested his left ankle on his right knee. He regarded the exposed length of sock; and when he had exhausted the sight of that he set the fingers of his left hand softly drumming on the desk.

'I'm in deep here, Jocelyn,' he said. 'This is the one I retire on; right? So what I won't want are the London relations muscling in.'

Coast had misjudged him. There had been a moment, too long a one, when he had thought that Peterson had been going to ask for more money.

'We've absolutely no intention of interfering,' he said. 'All we need is the man's name – and a small nibble at him, somewhere quietly at Heathrow, on his way through to Langley.'

'The name I don't have,' admitted Peterson. 'And I don't know who does. Like I wrote you, he's simply on the books as Minaret. And as for access to him on the way to Langley, that's between Whitehall and Washington.' He stretched an arm to reach the ashtray. 'In that direction, I can't help. Sorry.'

From somewhere downstairs music started up. After a few beats it stopped again.

Coast put on a smile with ice in it.

'You're not really being much help at all, Gus. Frankly. You are not, as we say, earning your crust.'

Peterson shrugged. It was a huge shrug. Most of his neck disappeared, turtle-like into the rolled collar of his pullover and both of his hands rose level with his shoulders in a gesture of defeat.

'Okay, Jocelyn,' he said. 'I owe. I'll tell you where I stand.' He stubbed out one Marlboro and lit another. He let a plume of smoke curl up by his cheek.

Where Peterson stood was like this: He didn't know who Minaret was, and he didn't care who Minaret was. From his point of view, the man was simply a precious consignment who had to be transported to Langley, Virginia, for de-briefing at CIA Headquarters. Peterson was going to escort him all the way. He was in charge. Right? Okay? Down to him were all the cars, the dummy documents, the rest-houses on the way, the smoke-screens. He had a crew, a bottomless sack of a budget, and a letter over a Presidential seal to commandeer any United States military or civil aircraft parked in any airfield in Europe. On this project he was omnipotent, answerable only to the Deputy-Director over at Langley. Right?

Coast made a show of being suitably impressed. It was clear that Peterson, in the winter of his career, felt that he had at last hit the big-time. He talked with enthusiasm, with gestures, swivelling his chair back and forth, built up a pyramid of ash and cigarette ends in the aluminium ashtray that advertised somebody's lager. There was no need to draw him out, his ego was doing that. All he had said so far was to put his name in bright lights; sooner or later he would come down to the mechanics.

He refilled the glasses. The music that had begun tentatively downstairs had now become more continuous for longer stretches. It had the slow insistent rhythm of bump and grind music.

There were two operations. Primary and secondary. The secondary, as its description implied, was a fall-back job. The thumb on the panic-button. Right? But that was a digression. More of that later. The chance of needing the secondary plan was only about one in ten. Long odds. So, okay; this was how he had set up the primary operation.

It was at this juncture that Peterson slid back his swivel chair and got briskly to his feet to reveal the first of the nuts and bolts. He shouldered the filing-cabinet to one side. Behind it, let into the wall, was a safe, about two feet high and a foot wide. Part key, part combination. The top shelf was jammed with passports and bank-notes, the second with envelope-files, the bottom with what looked like a CB radio and several other chunks of electronic gadgetry, together with a heap of large-scale maps. It was the latter that Peterson took out and dumped on the desk, and fanned out like a hand of cards. All these maps, his wife had said. All marked up with felt-tipped pens. All over the apartment.

Everything, the primary and the secondary plan for lifting out Minaret, hinged about Lubeck.

'Here,' said Peterson. An index-finger circled Lubeck, the south-eastern corner of Schleswig-Holstein, East Germany a few kilometres eastward, the Baltic Sea a few kilometres northward. Then Lubeck on a Baedeker guide, street by street, right down to the last detail, the police-station, the post office, the Buddenbrooks House in the Meng Strasse, that the tower of St. Peter's church could be reached these days by elevator. Circled in red felt-tipped pen was the first safe-house. It was near the Holstein Gate. In this safe-house, already equipped with a tape recorder and a telex with a direct line to Langley, and a computer programmed to encode, Minaret was to undergo his first de-briefing. Nothing exotic, nothing deep. Just insurance in case the KGB managed to hit Minaret between Lubeck and Langley. In the house by Holstein Gate, Minaret would make his first spill. Names, mostly. All the Centre's key-operators working out of Western Europe, then the smaller ones. These alone would be sufficient to break the Centre wide open. Could break it for years to come. And this alone would be ample repayment for the budget that Peterson had been allocated. Anything else was a bonus, the cream on the cake. Right? Sure as hell that's right!

Minaret was not going to be *hustled* out of West Germany. If the KGB knew their business, which they did sixty per cent of the time, they would have posses of operators out watching all the obvious exits. The harbours, the airports. Now the place to get lost in was a city. The needle in the haystack philosophy. They'd fixed on Hanover. Another map was unfolded, a small scale one; then, as it were, zooming-in, one to a larger scale. Business premises on the Winkelstrasse. The fourth floor. Just here.

Coast switched off at this point. His eyes saw and his ears heard, but he permitted himself to absorb nothing.

If Minaret was, in Peterson's jargon, going to be hit, Lubeck, even Lubeck, was going to be too late. He was going to have to be taken out before that. Long before.

Only by now, Peterson and his enthusiasm were unstoppable.

It took him an hour to exhaust himself.

He fell into his chair, then hunched eagerly forward over the desk, hands clasped tightly together, white-knuckled.

'What do you think?'

'Impressed,' said Coast. 'It looks like a smooth operation.'

Peterson frowned. 'Except what?'

'I'm not with you?'

'It looks like a smooth operation – you said. And then you were going to say except; right?' Peterson lifted his face querulously. It was a narrow face topped with a thatch of immaculately-barbered silver hair.

'Not at all,' Coast reassured him. 'It does seem to be a perfect operation. – So far as it goes; I was merely curious to know what happens before he gets to Lubeck. How he jumps the border, for instance.'

Peterson didn't know the answer to that, nor where Minaret was crossing over. No one did; except Minaret. Minaret had access to Soviet war-plans. According to Minaret, the million or so anti-tank and anti-personnel mines sown, according to Western Intelligence reports, down the East German border to hinder a NATO invasion, were not in every instance what they purported to be. Many were merely empty casings, without detonators, without explosive fillings. There were whole tracts like that, a hundred or more vehicles wide. Invasion-lanes for Warsaw Pact armoured divisions to roll over and break out into the West on the day of Armageddon. There were places, too, where the wire wasn't electrified. One only had to know where these were; and Minaret knew.

Minaret was coming into West Germany on his own, making his own way. He was just going to appear. Here. Peterson's forefinger tapped the map in front of him. Right here.

Right here was about twenty kilometres south of Lubeck. A black dot on the road through from Lubeck to Ratzeburg. Mildenheim. A black dot without a red circle about it. So its population was less than 2,000 and more than 1,000. So a small place. A village. A place where a man could not for long escape attention. Three – perhaps four – kilometres from the border.

This was the flaw he had been looking for, he was sure of that; although he said nothing to Peterson. He dropped Mildenheim into one of his cerebral files and rammed it home tightly.

Peterson collected Minaret at eight o'clock in the morning at the war-memorial in the centre of Mildenheim.

'You can be that precise?'

'Got to be,' said Peterson.

'So you must know the day as well.'

But to this Peterson shook his head.

'Not yet. I'm setting up the base at Lubeck at the end of next week. I hang out there until I get the word.'

The operation had been programmed into days, the days subdivided into hours. Hour One of Day One began at eight o'clock on an as yet undetermined morning beside the war memorial in Mildenheim. By Hour Two, operations would have moved north to Lubeck. The rest of Day One, and all of Days Two and Three would be spent in the house at Lubeck. On Day Four everything switched to Hanover.

Patiently, Coast guided Peterson back to Mildenheim, and reluctantly Peterson put aside his progress-charts and his acetate overlays.

'How the hell does he contact you from Mildenheim? Public telephone?'

'You've got it,' replied Peterson.

'How about taps?'

Peterson reached for his cigarette packet. 'Who's going to tap the telephones in a hick village in Schleswig-Holstein? Look, Jocelyn – .' He plucked two cigarettes from the packet and rolled one across to Coast. 'This operation is secure – bolted tight from the inside. Right? This character is KGB, I mean for God knows how many years he's thought, slept, and eaten KGB. *We* didn't choose Mildenheim. *He* did. He says he can get to Mildenheim; he says he can contact us from Mildenheim. He says don't fill Mildenheim with CIA heavies. He says I can make Mildenheim under my own steam without any trouble. Just send *one* man in *one* car to pick me up at eight o'clock on Day One in the square at Mildenheim. Okay, so this isn't the way we usually take a delivery. Right? But this is the way the man wants it; and who am I to argue with top brass from the K? Right?'

They lunched in the open air, on a balustraded terrace overlooking the Binnenalster Lake, the clatter of knives and forks and the buzz of a dozen half-heard conversations going on about them.

'What Whitehall wants,' Coast confided, tilting the wine-bottle over Peterson's glass, 'Is a meeting with this man. In transit, if you like. A couple of hours in a quiet hotel somewhere. Can you arrange that? At Heathrow, perhaps?'

'I've already told you, Jocelyn,' replied Peterson, waving his fork. 'Outside my terms of reference. Anyway, it might not be Heathrow. It could be Gatwick. I just don't know. You'll have to get your principals to take it up with mine.'

'We think,' said Coast, sipping at his wine. 'That your people intend to spirit him past our people without due notice. That you propose to milk him dry before we've even been allowed a look at him.'

This fabrication was only a hit or miss affair. It had no other purpose than to draw Peterson out further into vulnerability. But that it was a hit rather than a miss was made flesh by Peterson's evident discomfiture. He put down his fork and picked up his wine.

'You could be right,' he conceded. 'Not that we intend to snow your people, you understand – '

'Balls,' said Coast, sensing a new advantage. 'That's just what you intend to do.'

Peterson shrugged. Coast let him spike up a few more mouthfuls in silence, then said:

'I'll set a scene for you, Gus. Tell me what you think of it. – The immigration desk at Heathrow – or Gatwick – or wherever. Two men. One, a United States citizen with a perfectly satisfactory passport. He goes through. But the man with him – well, his passport isn't quite up to scratch. Incorrectly stamped somewhere along the line, perhaps; nothing too serious. But serious enough for this man to be taken aside and privately interrogated. For about two hours.'

'Then I contact Grosvenor Square and start a diplomatic incident.'

'But what if London made it worth your while?'

'Washington would find out in the end anyway,' said Peterson dismissively, but his interest had clearly been aroused. 'And there'd still be an incident.'

'Afterwards,' Coast reminded him. 'Not until afterwards.'

Peterson savoured that.

'Two hours?' he said.

'At the going rate,' proposed Coast. 'Whatever you think that is.'

A Position of Trust

Peterson hesitated only long enough to swallow the bolus of food he had been chewing.

'Hell, no,' he said. 'I'm not that stupid.'

They ambled slowly across Kennedy Bridge.

'I'm talking about a blank cheque, Gus.'

'Your people can't afford blank cheques,' countered Peterson, and underlined it by flicking his cigarette in an arc over the parapet.

'Try a figure,' said Coast.

Peterson took a few more paces, his shoulders hunched and his head lowered.

'Twenty-five thousand,' he said. 'Dollars.'

'Ten,' said Coast.

Peterson stopped and shot him a sharp sideways glance. 'So the cheque isn't that blank.' He started forward again. 'Twenty.'

'Fifteen.'

'Twenty,' said Peterson. 'Twenty and we've got a deal.'

'All right,' agreed Coast. 'Twenty. But paid on sight of the goods; unless you have any particular objections, that is.'

No. Peterson had no objections to that. His cheque was being paid into his Swiss account with the agreed regularity.

'But it had better be slick, Jocelyn. Nothing at that airport connects me with you and the Relations. Right? And if we smuggle Minaret out courtesy the United States Air Force, then you and I are out of it; and it's down to Washington and Whitehall. And we don't have a deal. Okay?'

* * *

He reverted to being Tavistock in the washroom of Dammtor railway station. At the DER kiosk on the concourse he bought a tourist-guide to Schleswig-Holstein, and several maps, at the largest scale they had, of its south-eastern corner. They were not the finely detailed Baedekers that Peterson had had, but for now they sufficed. In the restaurant, against a background of clattering crockery, train announcements and piped music, he spent a useful hour over them.

The eastern perimeter of Mildenheim was jammed hard up against the dotted line of the East-West border. A road, built, perhaps, before the war, cut the village in half in the west to east direction. Beyond the border it was marked as being disused, and petered out to a dotted line a few kilometres beyond the wire. A railway line that skirted Mildenheim's southern limits did the same.

The village was further bisected by the Travemunde-Lubeck-Ratzeburg road in the north-south direction. Thus it was quartered like a misshapen orange.

And it was there, he did not doubt, where the two roads crossed each other, east to west, north to south, that the square would be, and where the war-memorial was, and where Gus Peterson was going to collect Minaret on the morning of what he called Day One.

North of the village, the immediate north, was wooded. Further north it was heath and fen most of the way to Lubeck and the Baltic Sea. Open country. Yesterday he would have said that attempting to cross the border here would have been an act of sublime folly; but today he was no longer so sure. Peterson had sounded supremely confident of Minaret's abilities to defect unnoticed.

The thought was chilling. It could not, must not, happen the way Peterson had planned it. Somewhere between the north corner of Dzerzhinski Square and the war-memorial at Mildenheim, Minaret would have to be stopped. Terminally, if necessary.

But all that would be down to Michael and the mighty fist of the KGB. It would be out of his hands then. Michael was the one to tell. Michael would know what to do.

He dropped the maps and the guide in the week-end grip; and when the imminent departure of the train to Bremen and the Hague was announced he rose as if he were catching it and zipped the bag as he hurried out.

Eight

Michael was more sanguine.

He held up his fingers and numbered them off one at a time to register his points.

'One,' he said. 'To do what Minaret intends to do he would require assistance on *both* sides of the border. Two: that section of the border is monitored by sentries, radar and up to date infra-red detectors; which Minaret would know about if he is as highly placed as Peterson says he is. Three: only the Soviet General Staff has access to frontier-plans – what is genuinely mined and what is not. And, four: in a little place like Mildenheim Minaret would be as conspicuous as a gold tooth.'

'So what are you saying?' asked Coast tartly. 'That you don't intend doing anything about it?'

'No,' replied Michael. 'That is not what I am saying. – My point is that the operation is set up so crudely that it can only fail. I think your Minaret is one big bluff. A little man thinking tall; a filing-clerk perhaps, luring the CIA into thinking he is an important man. Not that he is any less dangerous from our point of view, I hasten to add. – Believe me, Anthony, he will not cross the border.' Michael stretched out an arm and closed a fist about an imaginary Minaret's throat. 'And if he thinks he can, he is a stupid little man.'

The reassurance was welcome, even if a little premature.

Then there were questions. Had Peterson ever mentioned the go-between who ran Minaret's errands to the CIA operators in Moscow? There had to be one. Was there a clue, a lead? Was the CIA already funding Minaret? Was Mrs. Peterson worth getting at? Was the Heider who owned the escort-agency CIA? Had Peterson said? Many questions, few answers.

The decoration of the flat was complete, the smell of paint gone. And with the heavy curtains up, and closed, there was no feeling of insecurity coming from the darkness over the heath tonight. There was even a sensation akin to cosiness about sitting here talking freely with this Michael; to be able to talk without prudence for once; and for a while, at least, not to be drawn into making the backward glance to see who was standing behind him.

'And have you progressed any further with the Lomax business?'

Coast shifted in his chair. The copy of the flimsy was still burning a hole in one of his filing-cabinets. Several times that day he had trod the passage in the direction of Lomax's office; but on each occasion he had passed by, even though he had known that Lomax had not been in there. Not only conscience – which he did not mention to Michael, – but cold reason also, had urged his footsteps on. He still felt that Lomax was too out of character for the role in which Quilter had whimsically cast him. By next week Quilter's attention might be focussed on Fanning or Templeton or someone equally more likely than Lomax could ever be.

But Michael insisted that a holding action must be put into operation soon, at once. If an opportunity had not occurred, then one would have to be engineered.

At ten o'clock on Tuesday morning he saw Lomax plodding towards the washroom with his newspaper.

He returned unhurriedly to his own office and took the copy of the flimsy from its cache among his files. He folded it twice across its width – it no longer mattered if his prints were all over it – lifted a trouser-leg and stuffed the paper down his sock. There was a rumble of voices from the Registry, but well inside it, and the corridor itself was empty.

Lomax's door was ajar. His briefcase was on the floor

beside his coat-stand. It was supple with age and scuffed at the edges and bore his initials in faded black script on the flap above the lock. Coast crouched beside it and assessed it, an ear cocked for any movement in the corridor. It was locked; the lock was a flimsy affair, probably easily sprung with a straightened-out paper-clip, but he didn't have time. The zip on the outer pocket was partly opened – and when he tried to open it further the zip was irretrievably jammed. Neither could he close it. He could just insinuate a couple of fingers. A quick feel about found only grit and what felt like a couple of bus-tickets. It was hardly a prime hiding place but it would have to do.

He took the copy from his sock and fed it in past the zip, the work of a moment, and he was back in his office several minutes before he heard Lomax go by in the opposite direction.

Quilter glanced pointedly at his wristwatch as he hurried into Coast's office and closed the door behind him.

'I hope this is quick, Jocelyn,' he said. 'I have a luncheon appointment.'

'Then I think you'd better cancel it, Tony.' Coast rammed his hands deeper into his trouser-pockets and clenched his fists tighter. It not only kept them out of the way but the pressure of his nails against the soft flesh of his palms gave him something tangible to concentrate upon. 'And I think you'd better sit down as well.'

'Don't be so bloody dramatic, Jocelyn,' Quilter snapped impatiently. 'I really haven't the time.'

'I'm sorry, Tony; I'm afraid you're going to have to make it.' Coast perched himself on the corner of his desk. The essence of everything now was a calm mingled with a grim fortitude.

'Tony,' he began, uncomfortably. 'About an hour ago I went through Eric Lomax's briefcase.'

In the ordinary course of events such an act was unforgivable. Briefcases here had the sanctity of a blind beggar's tin-cup.

Quilter's chin lifted.

'Go on,' he said. 'I'm listening.'

'I found a Xerox copy of a page out of one of his Adriatic files.'

Several expressions fleeted one after the other across Quilter's face. The last one, oddly, the one he tried unsuccessfully to hide behind a scowl, was of patent disbelief.

'Are you sure?' he said, still scowling. 'I mean, cast-iron? Absolutely?'

'Without a doubt. And it wasn't copied on our machine. Different watermark in the paper. I'm that bloody sure.'

Quilter found something of absorbing interest on the glossy black toe of his right shoe.

'How long ago?'

'An hour. Longer perhaps. I'm not sure.'

When Quilter looked up again the scowl had gone and anger had replaced it.

'An hour?' he raged quietly. 'An hour? Good God, Jocelyn, what the hell have you been doing in the time between? Sitting on it? Hatching it in the bloody hope it'll go away?'

'Damn it; of course I bloody haven't,' retorted Coast. Twenty years experience of constructing lies behind a blank expression now had to be unlearned. He rose and stood by the window looking down into Whitehall, and let his shoulders fall.

'Yes, I bloody have, Tony,' he admitted at last. 'I'm sorry.'

His dereliction of duty thus confessed, he turned and rested his behind against the radiator. 'Frankly,' he said. 'It was half in my mind to have it out with Lomax privately – and not report it to you at all.'

'Then I suppose we have to be thankful for small mercies,' Quilter said tartly. 'Personal loyalty is all very well – but for God's sake, Jocelyn, not at a time like this. Where's Lomax now? Do we know?'

'Lunch.'

'And with the briefcase – or without it?'
'Without it.'
Quilter stood aside from the path to the door.
'All right, Jocelyn. Bring the duplicate keys. Show me.'

The passage lay in the lunchtime quiet. At the far end, framed behind the arch of the Registry annexe, Heatherington sat at his desk eating his sandwiches and reading a newspaper. He paid them no attention, apart from one abstracted glance between a rustling of his pages.

Coast locked Lomax's door again – from the inside.

The briefcase was still on the floor beside the coat-stand. It appeared not to have been moved.

Quilter dropped to his heels beside it.

'Where exactly?'

'The zipped pocket. Facing you.'

Quilter gave the zip a tug.

'Jammed,' said Coast. 'It was earlier.'

Quilter made a beak of his fingers and felt about inside the pocket. For a moment it seemed that he was either missing what was there or Lomax had removed it. But then the folded copy came out clamped between two of his fingers.

He held it up.

'This it?'

'Yes. That's it.'

Still crouched there, Quilter quickly unfolded the sheet of paper and scanned it. The skin went white and tight on the bones of his face. He held the paper up to the light.

'What's the watermark in our paper?'

'A three-pronged crown. And our paper's thicker and whiter.'

Quilter rose. He went to the window and scanned the copy again in the better light.

Coast watched his back, trying to read the set of it; but it gave nothing away.

'You know what this means, Jocelyn, don't you?' Quilter said, at considerable length. 'It means that the original of this has already been out of the office.'

'I know,' said Coast. 'I'd already thought of that.'

Quilter turned grimly to face him.

' – And now I suppose it's the Special Branch, and the inevitable scandal.' He folded the piece of paper the way it had been in the briefcase. 'What an incredibly stupid thing for a man to do. Isn't it? Don't you think?'

The catechism continued.

'And neither of you had any concrete suspicions before this?'

The one called Fairhazel asked that one. He had declared himself a Detective-Chief-Superintendent from the Special Branch. No one had said what Tribe was, but Coast suspected he was MI6.

'I had none,' said Coast.

'And nor had I,' replied Quilter. 'Nothing, as you put it, concrete.'

'But you had something on him. A glimmering.'

'I was clutching at straws, Superintendent,' admitted Quilter.

'And how about you, sir?'

Fairhazel was sharp, a predator. Live eyes in a plump, languid face. His trunk and neck were the thick-set ones of a prop-forward.

'I had none at all,' replied Coast. 'Until Mr. Quilter asked me to keep an eye on him.'

It had been no sooner the word than the deed. Within ten minutes of Quilter's telephone call, Fairhazel and Tribe arrived together, and at one o'clock Mingay had joined them all in Quilter's office; although all Mingay had done so far was to prowl about like an overweight leopard and make the floorboards creak. It was still only ten past one.

'And he carried that briefcase every day?'

'So far as I remember.'

'Tell me, Mr. Coast ... ' This was Tribe, possibly the more dangerous of the two. ' ... don't you think it odd that a man who is going to steal a document, which he is obviously going to take out of the building in the evening, should chance leaving it in his briefcase while he goes out to lunch? I mean, would you do that?'

Coast smiled. It felt glassy. No one seemed to notice.

'I have absolutely no idea.'

The questioning passed back to Quilter. Tribe and Fairhazel bounced him between them like a rubber ball. It was all courteously informal, but not. Fairhazel looked half-asleep but was not, and Tribe affected not to be listening half the time and was. And in the darker cavities fear niggled and nerve-ends fretted together, because the betrayal of Lomax had been technically easy, but now the vultures were in and were going to peck every last shred of meat off the bones. Even Quilter wore a guilty look.

Then Coast was the ball.

Had he ever seen Lomax meeting anyone in suspicious circumstances? Did he ever leave the office at unusual times for no good reason? Stay on at night on his own? What keys did he have? The Registry, the strong room? Access to any safe other than his own? Keys to anyone else's office? – And this original, – and this really was the original, in its file open on Quilter's desk, a sheet of pink paper clearly once folded into eight to be smuggled out of the Registry –

' – Supposing someone had noticed it missing in the meantime?'

This was Tribe again. His tone was one of idle curiosity, no more than that.

'No one would – except Lomax.'

'Why?'

'Because only Lomax would need to; he has the Adriatic desk.'

'But *you* would have access to it – in the same way as Mr. Quilter would.'

'Yes. Of course. But I would never have noticed it missing unless it was something I was looking for.'

The floorboards creaked as Mingay continued to prowl.

There seemed no end to it.

'You've been checking on him every day, sir?'
'Yes.'
'And the briefcase every day, too?'
'Whenever it was there.'
'So it wasn't always handy?'
'He used it at lunchtimes – sometimes. Shopping, that sort of thing.'
'So he could have taken something out in it? At those lunchtimes?'
'It's possible.'
'Possible or likely?' Tribe, charmingly insidious. Dark suit, Dragoon Guards tie, the hewn sort of face that women liked.

'I'm not qualified to give an opinion.' The fretting nerves were making him sound truculent. He'd have to watch it.

'I'm sorry, gentlemen,' he said. 'I've known Eric Lomax for a long time. Sitting here like this gives me no pleasure. – As I'm sure it gives Mr. Quilter no pleasure.'

And Quilter agreed, and as soon as he opened his mouth the questions were switched to him again, and for a little while the heat was off.

It was a hectic afternoon. Affidavits had to be typed, and he and Quilter both had to sign them in the presence of two solicitors from the DPP's office. There was a horrible finality about doing that and the signature he usually dashed off had a distinct haltingness about it in too many places.

Twice, towards the later afternoon, Lomax came in to see him, blithely unaware of the time-bomb tucked back into his briefcase so that he could be caught in *flagrante delecto*, cheerful and boozy and wreathed in tobacco smoke.

They took him on the steps as he left at half-past six, quickly and without fuss after a single glance into the briefcase; one of the detectives kept hold of it while the other saw Lomax into the back of their car where a third one sat. And Coast tilted shut his Venetian blind as the unmarked car made a U-turn around the Cenotaph and joined the traffic heading up towards Trafalgar Square in the last of the rush-hour.

By seven o'clock the ghouls were in. Tribe, Fairhazel, and a new man called Prebble. They were coldly systematic. Quilter had asked him to stay behind and to keep an eye on them and to help in any way he could. His nerves craved a drink, but he had to settle for coffees from the machine along the corridor.

Lomax's desk was unlocked, the top drawer taken out and tipped empty over his blotter. The untidy heap was raked over, pens, pencils, rubbers, paper-clips, a drawing pin or two, a roll of Sellotape, and a lot of junk of the kind desks become heir to after their tenant has spent a decade at them. It was sifted through, sniffed at; a broken Shaeffer ball-point was unscrewed and taken apart. The scrap of folded paper in the barrel proved to be only the guarantee. The drawer was tapped, peered at, then slid back into the desk.

The second drawer held items of a more personal sort. A clean spare shirt professionally folded in a cellophane laundry packet; a spare necktie loosely rolled; a pair of new socks in a Marks and Spencer's bag; an electric razor and a brown glass bottle of trendy aftershave lotion with a black and silver cap. This last looked innocuous enough, but Prebble had the plastic cap off and sniffed at it, then again more keenly with flared nostrils. Then, between fingernail and thumbnail he prised out the plastic dropper and tipped a bead of the lotion on to the back of his hand and put the tip of his tongue to it.

'An alcoholic was he, Mr. Coast?'

'He may have been. Why?'

Prebble put back the dropper and screwed on the cap. 'This was his little store of vodka, sir. When they hide it like that it's usually a sign.'

While Prebble worked on the desk Fairhazel methodically plundered Lomax's bookcase. Every book was taken down, held by the spine and shaken. The more dubious looking ones had their pages flicked through. The cupboard underneath was emptied of its stack of old desk-diaries, Handsards and some out-of-date diplomatic almanacs. At the desk still, Prebble had taken Lomax's electric-shaver apart.

At midnight, Lomax's office looked as if it were waiting for a removal van to arrive. They wanted to open Lomax's filing cabinet, but Coast refused to authorise that and so, over the telephone, did Quilter. Only Mingay could sanction that, and Mingay at midnight could not be located.

Coast poured himself a large Haig. It was half-past one. He had come home by taxi.

There had been about the evening's work a relentlessness, a quiet and determined ferocity, almost a violence, as they had stripped Lomax's working life down to the bare bones. If they searched this place that methodically, they would expose him for what he was in less than five minutes.

He slept badly again, waking in the first few minutes of daylight and sleeping only fitfully after that until six-thirty when he rose, showered, shaved and dressed. The trip to Hamburg had broken his routine; he had got no groceries in over the weekend. A half-used loaf in the refrigerator had developed an unpleasant looking mould and the solitary slice of bacon that was left appeared no more appetising. He breakfasted on coffee and a cigarette, and wrote out a shopping list to use at lunchtime. There was nothing about Lomax on the news, nor in his morning newspaper. But then there wouldn't be yet. These were early days.

He was on the point of leaving for Whitehall, actually had the door open, when a thought struck him and he closed the door again and went through to the bedroom. At the wardrobe, he lifted a pile of underclothes and took out three of the cassettes of Kodak litho-film that he kept at hand for copying documents. He dropped two into one pocket of his jacket and one in another, and disposed of each in litter-bins on his way to the station. It had lightened the load a little; and in any case it would be months before he dared to copy anything.

* * *

He watched a pigeon swoop down from the top of the Cenotaph, then haul itself skywards again to flap across the roof of the Foreign Office. The hooligans were back and from Lomax's office came the occasional sound of a filing-cabinet drawer being opened and furniture again being shifted. And, as it had last night, their proximity pecked at too many raw nerves, made him wonder if he had left anything undone or done something that would have better been left undone.

The rap at his door startled him.

'Yes, Miss Goldring?'

'Mr. Quilter would like to see you, Mr. Coast.'

'Now?'

'He did say at once. He's in Mr. Franklin's office.'

He shrugged back into his jacket and lit a cigarette, and by the time he reached Franklin's room had put on a semblance of being back in control again.

Quilter was looking out of the window. When he turned, his face was ashen.

'You wanted me, Tony.'

Quilter motioned to him to shut the door, then, with what seemed a most tremendous effort, he raised a hand and drew a thumb and forefinger together across his eyebrows.

'I'm not quite sure if I'm waking *from* a nightmare, or into one, Jocelyn.' Then he paused and his hand fell back to his side. 'It's Lomax, Jocelyn ... He's dead.'

And for a moment there was silence. And for the moment after that Coast's stomach stirred uneasily as he found the ashtray on Franklin's desk. A welter of thoughts tumbled into his mind that seemed to have slipped temporarily out of gear. Yesterday Lomax had been hugely and lugubriously alive, and this was not the course events were supposed to have taken. Never for a moment.

'Christ ... how? ... do we know?'

'Oh, a heart attack ... something ... no one's sure yet.' Katerina Lomax had found him dead at about half-past six that morning. In an armchair downstairs. Their GP had guessed that Lomax had been dead for about two hours then. A wastepaper basket beside the chair was brimming with crumpled pieces of paper.

' ... his resignation, apparently ... he'd been drafting his resignation ... drinking, smoking, working himself up, I suppose.' Quilter patted his waistcoat distractedly for his cigarette-case, but had obviously left it in his office. Absently he took a cigarette from the packet Coast held out. In court yesterday evening Lomax's solicitor had asked for an adjournment, and had been granted one until this morning on condition that Lomax surrendered his passport. Only that.

'Not the happiest of circumstances, Jocelyn. ... I'm sure you'll agree.' Quilter had difficulty keeping the tip of the cigarette in the flame from Coast's lighter.

'Nothing else in that wastebasket? ... No clues ... no explanation?'

Quilter snatched a deep inhalation, and let the smoke seep slowly out again.

'I've no idea. I didn't ask. Frankly, it didn't seem the right time.'

Coast tucked his lighter back into his pocket.

'I suppose in a way it's down to us,' he said. 'Although if there was ever a prime candidate for a terminal coronary ... '

'Yes, ... well ... that's academic now, isn't it?' Quilter plucked a shred of tobacco from his lip. 'What's bothering me, Jocelyn ... at this moment ... is the fact that we might have been wrong about Lomax ... that we might have made a mistake ... just might.'

'Hardly, Tony. ... Do you think?'

'It isn't entirely impossible, is it? After all?' The colour was slowly returning to Quilter's face. 'Although God willing we may never know if we did or not.'

Coast made a tilt of his head towards the industrious sounds going on next door in Lomax's office.

'And what about those people?'

'Mingay's told them to carry on. And there'll be a full board of enquiry, of course. The mills of God; you know?'

Coast stubbed out his cigarette. He told himself, or tried to, that Lomax could just have easily died on his way home one evening, or during one of his lunchtime binges, today or tomorrow or next week. And if Lomax was only half proved innocent the boys next door would soon be looking for another scapegoat. They'd want the pack-leader, or whoever it was who had trailed the bait through the undergrowth.

'Do you want me to draft something?' That would be the next thing on the agenda. The death of Lomax would require the full panoply of Civil Service jargon to make it even remotely palatable across the street.

'A hell of a sight more than that, Jocelyn,' replied Quilter. 'I want every second of play the way you saw it – or even thought you saw it. No glossing over. No holds barred.'

'So you don't want a whitewashing job?'

'Definitely not.'

'For when?'

Quilter's cigarette followed Coast's into the ashtray. His thumb pressed down on it long after it was safely out.

'Mingay wants to read it this afternoon,' he said. 'Let's say noon, shall we?'

And then he turned for the door and impassively held it open.

'After you, Jocelyn,' he said. 'Twelve o'clock. And it had better be convincing.'

Back in his own office, Coast hung up his jacket. Then sat behind his desk and reached for a pad and pen; although he did not write a word for a long time.

Nine

The tape-recorded organ notes faded as Coast and Quilter left the chapel and stepped down on to the wet path. About them, voices rose and fell in cadences varying between self-conscious relief and hushed heartiness. Umbrellas were going up and mourners were gathering in uncertain little knots around the floral tributes laid out on the wet grass.

They joined the queue paying its respects to Mrs. Lomax, a short, lean, dark woman upon whom formal black sat all too well. Someone behind mumbled, 'Well, at least he's got the weather for it.' It had sounded like Toler.

A week had passed and the ghouls had moved on, and the Section was back in business again; although it was still the dead season and little was coming in or going out. It was also beset with the open sores of tribal mistrust. They had festered in the washrooms and in the lifts and on the stairs, and nothing went from hand to hand anywhere without a signature in exchange, and all the jokes were spy jokes, related with grim cynicism and received without laughter.

The nerve ends grated together less, but he still lived with the knowledge that he had cut it fine, and that Lomax, at least on an actuarial basis, might still be alive had he not been elected, on a whim, to head the list of expendables. It wasn't easy to live with that. He was all but finished. He had told Michael so. It would be a year before he could be useful again, and perhaps not even then. After the scandal that had swallowed Foster it had taken the Section the best part of two years to reassemble the pieces and knuckle down to work again. This was a smaller scandal, but while the sharp cries of outrage were still resounding among the Whitehall cobwebs a single puff of wind would blow it wide open.

'If you want anything, Katerina, get in touch won't you?'

'I shall, Jocelyn. Thank you.' After thirty years she was still Greek enough to wear a mourning veil. Her eyes behind it were strong and bright. When he tried to extricate his hand, her grip tightened and her umbrella tilted back and she closed a few inches. 'I need to talk to someone, Jocelyn. Someone Eric worked with. Can you come to the house?'

Rain dripped from the spikes of his umbrella. He had anticipated this moment last night, in bed, and shrank from it then.

'I have to get back, Kat. I'm sorry.'

'A few minutes here, then. Please, Jocelyn.'

Her fingers were immensely strong, her eyes as penetrating as Lomax's had been behind all that sleepy dogginess.

'Yes,' he said. 'Of course.' And only then did she let him go.

'I didn't know you knew her that well,' Quilter said, joining him by the flowers.

'She and Lomax were in Athens when Frances and I were.'

Quilter's umbrella tipped back and his eyes peered disapprovingly under its dripping edge.

'What did she want?'

'A talk. I could hardly refuse.'

'Well, for God's sake be careful.'

They stepped back on to the grass as another line of black limousines snaked slowly towards the chapel.

'Christ,' said Quilter. 'They can't churn them out fast enough, can they.'

After a few minutes Katerina Lomax came along the path and Quilter moved away.

'Remember what I said, Jocelyn. Be careful.'

She lifted her veil. Her dark good looks were still there. They had only aged.

'Thank you so much for waiting, Jocelyn.' She took his arm and they walked a few yards towards a sundial at the junction of two paths lined with rose-bushes. 'How is Frances – and the children.'

'They're well, Kat, thank you.'

They stopped by the sundial. Quilter had banded up with Toler and Franklin. All three were affecting not to be looking in their direction, but they were.

'It's a monstrous business, Kat,' he said. 'And there's nothing I can say to you; except that we're all deeply sorry. But I'm sure you know that.'

'He wasn't a spy, Jocelyn. He was an Englishman. The old kind.'

'There was evidence, Kat.'

'Yes. Eric told me. But such little evidence. He was sure that they could not convict him because of one sheet of paper. He said it was ridiculous. – They came to our house, you know, like Turks, and one was the same detective who came about the accident I was supposed to have had with the car. They pillaged our house, Jocelyn, and even when Eric had been dead for a week they came back and pillaged it again.'

'Kat, it's their job.'

'Eric died of sadness, Jocelyn, not from fear. He was betrayed; he told me that. They needed a scalp, he said, and they chose him. Your Mr. Quilter and your Mr. Mingay – or someone. He was to retire next year; he no longer mattered. All that he did in the war, all the work he did in Athens and Ankara – all that they must have chosen to forget.' She spoke with a quiet, controlled anger. Only the merest trace of Greek throatiness gave away her foreignness; and deep in her eyes was the knowledge that her every word was an undeniable truth; and practised dissembler though he was, he found it difficult to look at her. 'Jocelyn, I know only that I could not know about Eric's work. But I knew him. He was full of trust. He liked everyone.' There were tears now, but she controlled them. 'You have an expression, don't you? – The need to know.'

'Yes,' he said, knowing full well what her next question was going to be. 'We do say that. And I know what you're going to ask me, Kat. And I can't answer it.'

'Because you think the accusations were true?'

'Because we may never find out, Kat.'

'And if you do not find out,' she persisted. 'If nothing can be proved one way or the other; where will Eric stand then?'

'It's impossible to say. I only wish I could.'

'But *you* know, don't you, Jocelyn, the way I know? Eric was your friend. He was never a spy, was he? Was he?'

In her quiet wrath she had caught at his sleeve.

'Was he, Jocelyn?'

Lomax stood behind her shoulder, palpable but unseen.

'No, Kat. I really don't think he was.'

Her blackly gloved fingers fell away.

'At the enquiry – will you say that? Can you say that? Somebody must – even if the enquiry does not believe it. It is important for me; and important for Eric.'

The rain had stopped and the sun was coming out.

'Kat, I'll do what I can. I promise you.'

Theirs were the only umbrellas still up. From the tail of his eye he saw Quilter give his a brisk shake before shutting it.

'That a man should die on account of a single sheet of paper – that is not justice, is it?'

He pretended that Quilter had caught his eye.

'Kat, I have to go – '

'But you will speak for him?'

'I'll do what I can, Katerina.'

They walked back together and he shook her hand beside her waiting limousine.

'Give my love to Frances, won't you.'

'Yes,' he said. 'I shall.'

He took her elbow to help her in and saw her settled into a corner of the back seat.

'You'll be all right, won't you?' he asked. 'And I'm only at the other end of the telephone if you need anything.'

'Yes,' she said. 'I know that, Jocelyn.' She reached out her left hand for him to take.

He took it. He could feel her wedding-ring and engagement-ring hard under her glove. She looked very alone, very small. The man and woman standing deferentially nearby were her brother-in-law and sister who had flown in from Athens for the funeral. They looked ill at ease and slightly shabby.

'Rumour has it that Eric was writing his resignation,' he said.

She smiled sadly.

'Yes. A dozen times. So good with words. And he could not string enough together to tell them that he was finished with them.'

'Only his resignation?' he said. 'You don't think he put down any thoughts? Nothing constructive? No suggestions as to how that wretched piece of paper got into his briefcase? Nothing like that?'

Her hand fell away. She slowly shook her head.

'No,' she said. 'There was nothing like that. Nothing at all.'

That was more a relief to him than she would ever know. The contents of Lomax's domestic waste-paper basket had been like the nagging of a sore tooth since that morning in Franklin's office.

He took his foot off the door-sill and withdrew his head and shoulders from the grey interior of the limousine. 'Keep in touch, Katerina,' he said. 'Don't forget.'

'I shall, Jocelyn,' she said. 'Thank you.'

He stood aside for the sister and brother-in-law, and solemnly shook hands with each of them as they climbed in with Katerina; then sketched a last wave to her as the chauffeur shut them in.

'What did she want?' asked Quilter as he opened his umbrella. It was coming on to rain again. Toler and Franklin were walking on ahead. Franklin was going to phone for a Minicab.

'A word for Lomax at the enquiry. One can't blame her.'

'And will you?'

'I might. Depends how the wind blows.'

'Take my advice,' said Quilter, sidestepping a puddle. 'Don't. Sleeping dogs, Jocelyn; let 'em lie.'

By lunchtime Coast was back in his office and it was Friday; and last weekend had been like living alone on the top floor of a desolate tower block. He had been tempted to ring Frances, but he would only have received another token knee in the groin, and last weekend Lomax had been too newly dead for him to be able to break the news to her without giving himself away. So instead he had drunk too much; and read some Kafka with a curious willingness to identify himself with innocence caught up in the pincers of justice. But self-deception had never been his *forte*, and late on Sunday evening he had telephoned around the few women with whom he kept vaguely in touch and found one available. Paula, one of the hard drinking ones who treated sex like a dose of medicine and who demanded nothing afterwards but a few kind words of appreciation.

He rang her from the office at four o'clock; only this weekend, sorry pet, she was not available.

He had eaten on the way home; but it was still only eight o'clock on a bright evening and the new weekend was rearing up in front of him and the flat, if anything, had grown even smaller than last week. He tried reading, watching something inane on the television that only became more inane the longer he sat looking at it. He turned it off in disgust, only the silence was worse.

He knew that he ought to ring Frances and tell her about Lomax. He had asked the florist to write on the tag of his flowers: In friendship and affection, from Jocelyn, Frances, Simon and Susan; but a slip of someone's hand had turned Frances into Francis.

He finally picked up the telephone around ten o'clock.

A deep, male voice answered, and it took him a moment to remember that he was the father of a son old enough to have a regular girl friend, and who was far enough into puberty for even the very sound of him to have changed.

He belatedly twitched his smile into place.

'Simon,' he said, with a surprised heartiness. 'Hello – it's ...' It's who? Father? Dad? Daddy? Too much had changed too quickly. '... it's been a long time, old chap. How are you?'

There was a moment of awful silence. Then a woman's voice called 'who is it?', and Simon stage-whispered 'father' in reply.

'We're all well. Thank you.' Then, added grudgingly, 'How are you?'

'Oh, not so bad. – I was really after a word with Dizzy.'

'She's out. Rehearsal. End of term play.'

He shouldn't have rung. The stage-whispered 'father' had been another twist of the knife he could well have done without.

'You got the book, I hope.' The Walther pistol-kit was still in the car, he suddenly remembered.

'I already had a copy; last birthday. From you.'

The book had been a gaffe. He should have remembered. But on the other hand it had been churlish of the boy to be that outspoken. He had been too long alone with Frances and her insidious propaganda.

'Sorry, old chap. I must have had a blank spot. Send it back; I'll do my best to change it.'

'I already have. I did a swop.' There was no rise and fall to the voice, no inflection either one way or the other, simply a brusque boredom. 'And I'm not into guns any more. But thanks, anyway.'

O-levels and cricket proved to be equally fruitless avenues of conversation.

'Would you like to speak to Mother?'

'Yes, I would, old chap – if she isn't busy.'

He heard the telephone thud down on to the table. He shouldn't have rung. Every contact diminished him. The past was enemy territory.

'Hello, Joss.'

'Frances. – How are you?'

'Busy.' Crisp, incisive. Biting him off. She had been soft

once, as eager to have him between her legs as he was eager to be there, as often the initiator as he had been.

'I was wondering if I might come down tomorrow – take out Dizzy and the boy.'

'You mean Simon.'

'Yes,' he said tiredly. 'I meant Simon. I'm sorry.' They had never been close, he and the boy.

'It's inconvenient, Joss. I'm sorry.'

More than a silence. A stillness so total that the line might have been dead.

'Perhaps Dizzy could come over here then.'

'I'd rather she didn't.'

Anger rose.

'I've still got bloody rights, you know, Frances.'

'Why now? You've had them for six years. – You should have used them.'

'Anyway, what's so bloody inconvenient about tomorrow?'

They were all going over to Reading, to see Donald's elderly mother.

' ... Try next week end.'

'I might be busy next week end.'

'That's up to you, Joss, isn't it.'

He swallowed his temper. Of necessity. Loosing off now would only make it worse the next time he rang her.

'I'm sorry, Frances,' he said, a metaphorical touching of the forelock, the words bile on the tip of his tongue. 'A bad day at the end of a bad week. Sorry.' Now was the time to mention Lomax; only he couldn't. 'If it's all right, I'll give you a buzz next week.'

Her mood had stayed as it was. He could sense that even though she hadn't uttered a sound.

'I'll try to keep next weekend free,' she said, eventually. 'But don't bank on it.'

He smiled tightly as he bade her goodbye, and slammed the receiver down the cradle with the smile frozen off his face. Fran and Jo-Jo they had been once, on beds, on sofas, on cushions in front of the fire, in a riotously happy world that wasn't going to end because they weren't going to let it. Except that it had, not with a bang or a whimper, but in this cold lifeless silence.

Quilter rang him late on Sunday evening.

He didn't answer at once. His tongue was thick in his mouth and his eyelids felt gummed together, and further testimony to his dull-headedness was the more or less empty bottle standing on the sideboard with a dirty glass beside it.

'That *is* you, isn't it, Jocelyn?'

He shoved a hand through his hair and brought his brain to order.

'Yes, it's me. Sorry, Tony. I was asleep.'

Quilter apologised for waking him; but it was, he thought, important.

'It's Middlecheap,' he said. 'Mingay's just rung to tell me.'

Middlecheap and Rosmer were the two QC's short-listed to preside over the enquiry into the Lomax affair. The grey eminences had settled for Middlecheap.

'But he's politically left, surely?'

'I don't agree with the choice either,' replied Quilter sourly. 'But Mingay seems to think it might be better that he is. Less chance of him papering over any cracks, as it were. I can't say I go along with him; but there it is.'

The morning sun filtered into Tribe's office through a haze of cigarette-smoke. Tribe sat behind the desk, Quilter, Coast and Fairhazel in front of it, and Clive Mingay, wearing a pale grey suit that he fitted like a prosperous bookmaker, sat with one bulging thigh on the window ledge with one pink sock revealed between the bottom of a trouser-leg and one grey suede shoe. The window itself gave on to the unlovely hind end of Charing Cross railway station.

The centre of attention was presently Fairhazel, his notebook at his elbow on Tribe's desk to refresh his memory. He had begun at the beginning and was about to describe his illicit entrée into Lomax's household.

'I trust you were subtle,' broke in Mingay. 'Nothing that'll bounce back on us.'

'No, sir,' replied Fairhazel. 'I borrowed his car for ten minutes and nudged it into a tree. I doubt he'd even have claimed it on his insurance.'

Coast chalked up a mental mark for himself. He had guessed the car incident had been carefully scripted.

'As a man, Superintendent,' prompted Tribe. 'What did you think of him?'

Fairhazel rolled his lower lip forward consideringly as he reached for the ashtray.

'He was an alcoholic,' he said. 'And that's for sure. But otherwise a gentleman of the old school. Nice home. Fond of his wife.'

'Clever, do you think? Devious enough to lead a double life?'

'I wouldn't put money on it,' said Fairhazel.

'Want facts, Tribe, not opinions,' Mingay broke in waspishly from his vantage point on the window ledge.

There was a moment of silence.

'How about his bank account?' asked Quilter hopefully.

It was overdrawn; and on the mantleshelf of the Lomax dining-room had been a bill for rates and another for the telephone, both printed in red, both final demands. And the tax-disc on the borrowed car had only been a six-monthly one.

'So he was broke,' proposed Tribe.

'Yes, sir,' agreed Fairhazel. 'I'd say he was.'

'Anything going into his bank – other than his salary?'

'No, sir. Nothing.'

'Perhaps they were paying him in cash,' suggested Quilter.

'Who?' enquired Mingay, scowling.

'Whoever he was working for.'

'Oh, I see,' grunted Mingay, and switched his gaze back out of the window.

'If he was working for anybody at all,' ventured Tribe. 'And personally I don't think he was.'

'Well somebody bloody well was,' said Mingay, still scowling out of the window. His contributions to the subject in hand had so far been few, and his occasional blustering outbursts had sufficient of the bully in them to reduce the rest of the gathering to silence.

A train horn blared distantly, and the sonorous tones of Big Ben struck the quarter after eleven.

'We've got a Magnitude Nine balls-up on our hands,' proposed Mingay, breaking the silence he had generated. He looked querulously at each of them in turn. 'That *is* what we're all saying, isn't it? That we jumped the bloody gun. That we all think Lomax was our man and haven't got more than a shred of evidence to prove it.'

'I still don't think he *was* our man,' said Tribe, correcting him.

Mingay glowered down at the back of Tribe's head.

'I'm accountable to elected politicians, Tribe. They aren't interested in what we *think*. It's what we *know*. And what we know is that one of Quilter's people was caught bloody red-handed taking out a certain document from his office one evening.'

'And that's all we know,' countered Tribe.

'Great God,' said Mingay. 'That's enough, isn't it? Can't we build on that?'

'We've tried,' said Tribe. 'And all we've done is to reach a dead end.'

Fairhazel lit a cigarette, an act that spread around the gathering like a virulent plague.

Mingay's impatience erupted again as he put his lighter away.

'We've got to get our act together. – That list of frequencies was found in the street in Lomax's briefcase. I mean *that's* a bloody fact.'

No one answered.

'So we're all agreed on that. The list was a copy. Xeroxed. Made somewhere outside Quilter's office. Also a fact.'

There were, this time, a few tentative nods of agreement.

'And it didn't get into his briefcase by accident. Agreed?'

And for a few moments, again, his voice and his bulk dominated the room and quelled it to silence.

'And that's what Middlecheap hears,' he said. 'No opinions, no expressions of sympathy from loyal colleagues, just facts. Have we got all that?'

Coast and Quilter slowly circumvented the array of empty deckchairs around the bandstand in St. James's Park.

'I think Mingay's right,' said Quilter. 'I think we have a copper-bottomed case. Everything points to Lomax.'

'Unfortunately,' agreed Coast. It was time to withdraw. Lomax was dead; no more harm could come to him.

'What I'm trying to say is,' Quilter said, looking down at the grass as if something unpleasant had caught his eye among the daisies. 'That you won't be voicing any protestations of Lomax's innocence. Because it won't do any good, you know. You won't be doing that, will you, Jocelyn? Not now.'

No, he would not. The course was set. If he had done nothing else he had purchased time. Investigations would be well under way in Moscow by now. They would be more thorough there.

Ten

June had slipped uneasily into July, and for a few hours they had conjured up Lomax from the dead.

You've never seen that piece of paper before, Mr. Lomax?
Never.
But this original. You've seen that before?
Yes, I have. The Adriatic zone is my particular brief.
And who would have filed it?
I would have done that myself.
You can see that it's been folded at some time?

A rustle of paper came from the loudspeaker of the tape-recorder as the flimsy changed hands. The interrogator was clearly Tribe.

Yes, I can.
Why?
I have – honestly – no idea.
You were with SOE during the war. Working with Greek partisans.
Cretan partisans; yes, I was.
Communists?
And brigands and smugglers. At the time we made little distinction. – And here Lomax permitted himself a little irony. – We were singularly hard pressed for friends in those days, you see.

There were advances, retreats. There were casual asides and by the ways and the constant repetitions of seeming irrelevancies. Except that Lomax was too old a dog.

Why do you think those folds are there, Mr. Lomax?

I've told you, Colonel. I *don't* know.

In the occasional passages of silence a soft, metallic, rhythmic clicking came from the mechanism of the tape-recorder.

Did you take it out of the building at any time? Perhaps to copy? Might that be a reason for these folds.

I did not.

At the far end of the table, beyond the slowly ticking tape-recorder, sat Middlecheap, his hairless head gleaming in the pearly light from the window behind him. With both hands he was clutching a pencil across the lower half of his face; and through the lozenge-panes of the leaded window the tower of Big Ben was shattered into a distorted mosaic. Mingay, as was meet, sat at the opposite end of the table with Quilter on his right and Coast on his left, and Tribe, as was also meet, sat at the middle to make plain his impartiality in this matter. Opposite him sat Fairhazel, so immobile that he might have been dead.

You must have made a number of Communist connections.

Oh, yes. Dozens. And for a number of years the Foreign Office paid me to do so. It's a strange dark world, ours, Colonel. Much like yours, I should think.

Perhaps you still make contact with one or two? Do you? Where did you copy this, Mr. Lomax?

For the first time Lomax was tripped. The one question had clearly come while he was still framing the answer to the other.

Copy what?

This. – A slap of fingernails against a sheet of paper. A touch of violence, only a small touch, and vicarious at that, but violence all the same. *This*, Mr. Lomax.

I've already told you; I didn't.

A much longer pause this time; Lomax most likely cleaning his reading glasses with the end of his necktie.

That copy *was* in your briefcase, Mr. Lomax.

Then it was put there by someone else.

Who?

Colonel – I have absolutely *no* idea.

Mingay scribbled something on his jotter and twisted it for Quilter to see, then drew it back again.

GETTING NEEDLED, Coast read.

Do you know any of these people, Mr. Lomax? – Take your time.

Middlecheap aimed a finger at the tape-recorder. Fairhazel reached out and paused the tape. The clicking stopped.

'What were you showing him, Colonel Tribe? Photographs?' A lapidary style, each word separately hewn by a voice pitched to carry. Too loud and too highly pitched for this small room above Parliament Square.

'A book of faces, Mr. Middlecheap. Soviet consular staff – journalists – trade delegates.'

'And he recognised none, of course.'

'On the contrary, he recognised several. From his days in Ankara and Athens.'

'But a pointless exercise, Colonel? I mean he was hardly likely to point out any he knew currently. If, that is, he did.' Middlecheap motioned to Fairhazel to start the tape-recorder again.

For a long time there was only the steady tick, interrupted every so often by the turning of a page.

'If this is Lomax looking at your photographs, Colonel, I suggest we speed it up a little.'

Fairhazel depressed a key on the panel of the recorder; released it as the loudspeaker suddenly loosed the sound of fighting tomcats; carefully inched the tape back a few inches.

You know this is ridiculous, don't you, Colonel Tribe?

Lomax was to repeat this theme, with variations, four times during the next twenty minutes. By turns he tired, was hostile, was petulant, was scathing.

If your people had been more competent, Colonel, they'd have arrested me *after* I had handed this bloody thing to whoever the recipient was supposed to be. *Not* before.

And were you going to do that, Mr. Lomax?

Don't talk bloody wet! If you had thought I intended to, you'd have put a tail on me.

'He's right. Why didn't you, Colonel Tribe?'

Fairhazel once more reached out to stop the tape-recorder.

'Because my instructions from my superiors were to the contrary, Mr. Middlecheap.'

Mingay came to life. He tossed down the pencil he had been doodling with and leaned back in his chair.

'They were my instructions. This leakage of information had been going on for a long time. I wanted it stopped. And if we had had Lomax followed, and hadn't been able to intercept that list before he passed it over we would have been party to treachery ourselves. We can't arrest Soviet diplomats, Mr. Middlecheap.'

Middlecheap scrawled something, and manifested his displeasure by terminating his note with a heavily stabbed full stop.

The winds of Lomax's anger buffeted into the darkest corners of the narrow, panelled room. He was no longer cautious, had passed long since any desire to weigh his answers before he uttered them. It had been, perhaps, too many hours since he had last had a drink. His voice shook with outrage.

Then why don't you arrest me? Why don't you bloody well charge me?

There was no reply. Lomax's anger gusted stronger.

Who are you in with, Colonel? What bloody phoney game are you playing, eh?

What was that list *doing* in your briefcase, Mr. Lomax?

Ask whoever put it there. – And I refuse to answer any more of your bloody questions, Colonel Tribe. You either release me now or charge me.

Outside, it was raining and the sound of traffic was louder.

Coast glanced from face to face as the opportunity arose, the odd man out here, the only one who did not fit in. Of the six around the table, only he knew without doubt that Lomax did not have a shred of treachery in him, was incapable of the clandestine meeting, the furtive handovers in crowded Tube-trains and the backs of taxis. Lomax had been possessed of lugubrious innocence; but these men, mercifully, knew nothing of that.

The afternoon dragged sluggishly to its close.

'What we have to ask ourselves,' proposed Middlecheap, 'Is whether or not Lomax had a case to answer. Was there – in fact – a case at all? We don't know. Did Lomax intend to communicate what was found in his briefcase to an agent of a foreign power? We don't know that either; and probably never shall. Was Lomax, as he himself intimated, a victim? If he was, then whoever the traitor is – or was – he or she might still be operating. If he was not a victim, then it is possible that he *was* a traitor.'

Pausing, Middlecheap took up the transcript of the proceedings in the magistrates' court and brandished it by his cheek. His hair had not so much thinned as vanished. Or perhaps he had never had hair at all.

'Adjourned pending further evidence. Suspended from duty, passport withdrawn. – The outcome of inadequate evidence.' Putting down the transcript he then picked up the coroner's report on Lomax. 'And perhaps a further outcome,' he said weightily.

Coast sent a glance towards Quilter, but Quilter was looking impassively along the table at Middlecheap. Mingay had finished doodling arrow-heads and was making a long note with several key-words underlined.

'Has anyone anything to add?'

'Yes,' said Mingay, with a sudden and unexpected passion that had everyone startled for a moment. It was another moment before Mingay deigned to raise both his eyes and his face from his pad.

'I have,' he said. With consummate care he laid his propelling-pencil alongside his pad, leaving a finger delicately poised on the barrel in case it decided to roll away, and only taking it off when he was completely sure that it wouldn't; and only then when he was sure that he held everyone's attention undividedly.

'Supposing there is no further evidence, Middlecheap?'

'Then the most he could have been charged with was theft. – But that isn't my business, Mr. Mingay. My brief is to assess all the known facts and uncover what others I might find during that exercise. – And since Mr. Lomax is now beyond the law, official interest lies only in the fact that he was either a spy or a go-between for a foreign power; or that he was not.'

'And what can you do that Tribe already hasn't?'

'My powers are wider, Mr. Mingay. I have *carte blanche* from the Secretary of State to come and go from any of your departments as I see fit. And it is my intention to question everyone who is even remotely concerned in this affair – from the Secretary all the way down, if necessary, to the people who empty your dustbins.'

Middlecheap then glanced at his watch, a steel braceleted digital model, more in keeping with a fighter-pilot's image than the staid possesser of chambers in Grays Inn, thus disposing of Mingay as plainly as if he had shut a door on him.

'Has anyone else anything to say?'

No one had.

'Very well. Since this is only a preliminary meeting I shall only be sending a copy of the minutes to the Secretary of State; anyone wishing to examine them may apply to him.' A brief flourish produced a diary from inside his jacket. 'Colonel Tribe, I should like to come and talk privately with you next Monday morning at ten o'clock. Suitable, is that? Or not? – Good. Thank you. Mr. Mingay at the same time on Tuesday. – And you, Mr. Quilter, I shall telephone when the need arises to make an appointment. – And you, Mr. Coast, I understand to be my guide and adviser.' And, astonishingly, suddenly and brightly, Middlecheap's square, pugnacious face lit with a smile. 'In short, you are to liaise with me at the expense of any other work you might have for the time it takes to sort this business out. I take it you're agreeable?'

By night, Quilter's club was gloomier than ever, and the *salle privée* the last solitary outpost of a decaying empire waiting for the rabble to come in and take it over.

Quilter gathered cracker crumbs into a neat pile with the back of his knife, then heaped them on to an already buttered cracker. He topped it off with the last of his cheese. Rain still dripped from the trees in the Mall.

'I'm not sure I'm qualified,' Coast said.

'You knew Lomax better than anyone. And for longer, too, come to that.' Quilter's teeth nipped a crescent from the corner of his cracker.

'And that disqualifies me,' Coast insisted. 'It makes me an interested party.'

'Rubbish, Jocelyn.' Quilter's adam's-apple rose and fell again as he swallowed. 'I'd say you were better placed than anyone to persuade Middlecheap to think along the right lines.' Quilter's cracker floated up towards his waiting teeth once more, but stopped short a few inches away. 'Personal loyalty is all very well,' he said sharply. 'But it has to stop when treachery is involved. – Bugger all the legal palavering; that list was found in Lomax's briefcase. It wasn't found in yours or mine or Fanning's or Toler's. It was found in Lomax's. And for God's sake, man, you were the one who found it there.'

'I'm still not convinced he was guilty, Tony.'

'Then, with respect, Jocelyn, you're the only one who isn't.'

He felt himself treading deeper into the maze. The Section was beginning to oil its wheels and prime its engines. Another week or two would see it fully back in business; although he would not be, even though Michael had promised him that any further information to Moscow would go by another route and finish up on a desk in an entirely different Directorate. Interrogations were going on in Dzerzhinski Square at a great pace in an effort to spike Minaret where he sat. He could not come across. The odds were now too great. Peterson would bide forever in Lubeck waiting for him. The KGB was as ubiquitous as it was omnipotent. Minaret would be located; and Michael had traced a line about his own throat with a forefinger to demonstrate the short shrift that his superiors meted out to KGB personnel who fouled their own nests.

And in any event it was going to be several months before he got his nose back into the working-trough. Orders had come down through Mingay that security arrangements were to be tightened in every possible direction. The old ways were to be thoroughly investigated. What was effective about them was to be dusted down and kept in use; what was not was to be ruthlessly cast out and replaced.

'He proposed you, Jocelyn; a sort of one-man commission. Sniff around, see what you can come up with. No hurry. Take your time. Get it right.'

It had all been done before. Only in a perfect world would security ever be perfect.

'What news of Peterson?' Quilter asked suddenly. 'Anything?'

'Nothing,' replied Coast.

'He seems to be getting a hell of a lot of money for precious little output. Do you think he's on the up and up? I ask because Mingay's beginning to press.'

'Sure he is,' Coast assured him. 'I told him we weren't interested in gossip. Only quality goods.'

'Quite right. – Only Mingay considered that we should have given Peterson a small retainer and made him further payments by results.'

There could be no doubts about Peterson, certainly at this stage of the Minaret operation.

'Do you want me to chase him?'

'No,' said Quilter. 'That wouldn't be wise. Don't want to upset him, do we?'

The next week was notable only for its feeling of anticlimax. The cars were all in their places on the starting-grid but the raised flag did not come down. He lunched several times with Quilter, and on one of those occasions tentatively broached the subject of Minaret. There had been a couple more drips, according to Washington, but nothing that anyone could authenticate. It was even possible that the Russians might have taken him out, and tried to substitute someone else in his place who would disseminate misinformation to order. Washington had become decidedly withdrawn on the matter of Minaret.

But when, on the Sunday afternoon, he telephoned Roma Peterson in Paris she told him that so far as she knew Peterson was still in Hamburg; and, more importantly, that he was more or less incommunicado, even to her, even in the direst emergency.

'And how are things with you?'

'Oh,' he said. 'You know. Busy.'

'Too busy to come over?'

'Yes,' he said. 'Afraid so.'

'Pity.'

He laughed. Roma Peterson could drum a lot of mileage out of a couple of syllables of innuendo. A month ago he would not have cared if he never saw her again; but the world was getting on top of him lately and the sound of a woman, even of her, was like a squirt of nicotine straight into the arm.

And then Monday again, the sharp end of the week.

'Scissors, Miss Spencer?'

'Scissors, Mr. Coast.'

'Six pairs?'

'I thought my girls ought to have a pair each. – Make each responsible for her own pair. ... People keep coming in and borrowing them; and they simply *don't* come back.' She pushed the chitty closer across the desk and dared him not to sign it.

And at eleven he was along in Quilter's office and Mingay was there demanding a security so tight that even a ferret couldn't wriggle through it.

Then on Tuesday Middlecheap appeared. Wesley was moved along to Lomax's erstwhile office to make way for him and by lunchtime Middlecheap was firmly ensconced with only a connecting door between himself and Coast. During the afternoon a tape-recorder was installed for him, and a telephone that did not connect with the switchboard along the passage but which went directly out of the building.

With his coming, rumour succeeded rumour. For several days he appeared to do nothing but shuffle papers. He was in the office long before the rest of the Section arrived and left long after them. Not until Friday did he finally emerge and ask Coast to take him on a tour, make a few introductions, that sort of thing. His demeanour was hail-fellow-well-met. He rubbed the palms of his hands together frequently, and Coast soon learned that this was not a sign of affability but that Middlecheap was in a hurry. Fanning nicknamed him the White Rabbit.

He began in the Registry on Friday afternoon. Where were the files kept? How were they graded? Who had access to what? What particular cages did Mr. Lomax have access to? Heatherington trailed after him with evident wariness. This was his domain and he governed it according to the rules laid down by Mr. Quilter and Mr. Coast.

'I'm not looking into any dereliction on your part, Mr. Heatherington.' And Middlecheap patted Heatherington's sleeve. 'Really. Show me the strong-room, will you.'

He approved of the strong-room, waddling down to the far end of it, then hoisting the tail of his coat so that he could plunge his hands into his trouser-pockets while he looked about.

'And did Mr. Lomax have free access here as well? I suppose he did.'

'Not entirely unrestricted,' Coast said. 'He would have got a chitty from either myself or Mr. Quilter.'

'But he would – could – have come in here alone?'

'Yes, indeed.'

Middlecheap waddled back. What he lacked in height he more than made up for in width. He tested the weight and swing of the door as a matter of private interest.

'How about your wastebaskets? Shades of Dreyfus; that sort of thing.'

'Mr. Heatherington clears them out every afternoon at

five thirty. We shred everything.'

'And the shredded waste? What happens to that?'

Heatherington showed him the sealed plastic refuse-sacks beside the Xerox machine.

'And you do this every Friday? And a security firm takes it away for incineration?'

'Yessir.'

Middlecheap led the way back to the hardboard chicane and Heatherington's desk. Heatherington showed him the procedure for booking documents out of the Registry and how copies were recorded.

'But not entirely foolproof,' suggested Middlecheap, turning pages with an intensity that hinted that he was looking for a specific entry. 'Without someone like yourself to supervise it?'

Heatherington pondered that, his very nature rejecting the implied flattery and causing him some confusion while he weighed his reply.

'It has to be operated properly, sir. But mostly it works.'

'So it isn't foolproof,' said Middlecheap, but moderating the chide with one of his vivid smiles. 'Tell me, Mr. Heatherington,' he hurried on while Heatherington was still gathering his frown together. 'How well did you know Mr. Lomax. Very well?'

Heatherington's military rectitude at last came to the fore. He drew himself taller and squared his shoulders and lifted his chin, so that his grey gaze was directed sharply downward to fix on Middlecheap's upward one.

'No, sir. I can't say I did.'

Middlecheap's amicable veneer was not quite as substantial as it appeared. He rubbed his hands together briskly as if he were dusting sand off his palms.

'Yes. Well. We'll have to see.' Still rubbing, but slower, he tipped his head upward and sideways to Coast. 'I'd like a word with Mr. Heatherington, Mr. Coast. In private. Do I have your permission?'

'Do you want me to sit in?'

'No, thank you,' replied Middlecheap curtly. 'I shall be in

Mr. Wesley's office, Mr. Heatherington. – Lock up, won't you. Don't want any more sheets of paper slipping out of sight beneath the wainscot, do we?' And on this note of topical banter his silhouette receded down the passage and gave the illusion that it passed through the wall as it went into Wesley's office and the door closed behind it.

'What do I say, sir?' asked Heatherington, a rare note of awkwardness in his voice. 'I mean I don't know anything about all this business, sir. Not a thing.'

'No one thinks you do, Mr. Heatherington. He'll ask you a few questions and you'll do your best to answer them. We don't expect you to do more.'

When Coast left his office at six-thirty, Middlecheap and Heatherington were still closetted together in the room next door and showing no sign of coming out, even though it was the weekend.

Eleven

Fanning strolled with him towards the refreshment marquee. It had so far been a fine afternoon; but towards the west grey clouds with vividly luminous edges were rolling closer, and from time to time a rumble of thunder came their way like a barrage of distant artillery. From the adjacent meadow floated the occasional sound of willow against leather and rounds of desultory hand-clapping.

'I would say unequivocally,' observed Fanning drily. 'That our young Wesley hasn't done at all badly for himself.'

'She'd frighten the hell out of me. Wesley'll be in chains within a week; the way she spat out those responses. Bloody alarming, I thought.'

The inside of the marquee was like a greenhouse. They joined a queue of morning suits and carnations at a long trestle table where drinks were being dispensed. Something unpleasantly soggy underfoot was a cream-filled pastry, clearly recently dropped by a little page-boy whose frilled shirt was being hastily mopped down by his elegantly clad mother. The Section was here *en fête*. Fanning's wife, and Toler and his wife, were chatting away in the far corner of the tent. Quilter, looking as harrassed out of Whitehall as he did in it, was bearing down on the group around Templeton, Mrs. Quilter hard behind him.

They took their drinks back outside where it was marginally cooler. As weddings went, this one had gone with commendable smoothness. Miss Spencer had arrived on her father's arm within seconds of the appointed time, replied 'I do', in clear ringing tones that boded ill for Wesley's future, and was presently marching around like a young grenadier with a beaming Wesley in her wake. Marriage had clearly invigorated her.

'How are you getting on with the White Rabbit?' asked Fanning. 'Pushing you hard, is he?'

'He's looking for absolutes; and I don't think he'll find any.'

'You sound pretty convinced.' Fanning sipped at his drink, his eye on a couple of bridesmaids who were playing with the Spencer's golden retriever on the grass beside the ornamental fishpond.

'It's too late,' Coast said. 'If there were tracks they'd have found them by now.'

The retriever bounded into a garden chair and sent flying a grey top-hat and a pair of grey gloves that had been left on it.

'The White Rabbit asked me if I thought Lomax was a pinko – or a fellow-traveller,' said Fanning. 'Bloody ridiculous; I told him.'

It was another Monday of another week. Middlecheap had sifted through most of the staff and this was his grand finale.

'How long have you been Mr. Quilter's Deputy, Mr. Coast?'

'Four years.'

'Since Mr. Quilter became Head of Section; more or less.'

'The same week.'

Middlecheap's finger and thumb toyed with a corner of Coast's dossier that he had to hand on Wesley's desk.

'The two of you were put up together, I understand; for the post Mr. Quilter presently fills.'

'It's all in there,' Coast said. 'I'm sure you've read it.'

Middlecheap glanced down at the dossier, looked as if he was about to open it; but then slid it aside in the manner of a man who would much prefer to hear everything from the horse's mouth, as it were.

'Must have irked you a little,' he said. 'Mr. Quilter in the pilot's seat, while you were half a dozen doors away along the passage.'

'Not at all,' replied Coast, careful to inject into his voice the same casual bonhomie that Middlecheap was using. 'He'd had more administrative experience than I had had. It was a sensible choice.'

'And you were also in the throes of divorce proceedings, I understand.'

'Yes, I was. Although I don't think that had anything to do with it.'

Middlecheap smiled.

'No,' he agreed. 'I'm sure it didn't.'

And you're foxy, thought Coast.

'Tell me, Mr. Coast, who or what put you on to Lomax?'

'Mr. Quilter.'

'You had no thoughts of your own? Nothing that would cast suspicion elsewhere?'

'Nothing that I could possibly substantiate.'

Middlecheap savoured that.

'You're saying, I think,' he proposed. 'That you might have looked elsewhere if Mr. Quilter had not mentioned his doubts about Lomax. That right?'

'Yes. I think so. I'd known Lomax for a long time. We struck up a friendship when my wife and I first went to Athens. In 'sixty-two.'

'A friendship that you maintained?'

'Until my divorce.'

Middlecheap frowned.

'You mean the two of you quarrelled?'

'No, I don't.' Coast took out his cigarettes. 'Do you mind ... ?' Middlecheap pushed an ashtray across the desk. 'Friends eventually accept a married couple as a single unit. And after a divorce they aren't quite sure whether to invite one half of the unit without the other constitutes a disloyalty to the other half.'

'Ah,' said Middlecheap. 'I do see.' He slid his chair forward a few inches on its castors and propped his elbows on the desk. 'So you stayed friends, but ceased to be – shall we say – close companions?'

'Yes.' Coast let his lighter snap shut and exhaled.

'Exactly.' He felt very cool, very calm, very under control. Middlecheap was taking it leisurely. So would he.

'I can't imagine it was pleasant for you, then, to be asked to keep a close eye on him?'

'It wasn't.'

'And even more unpleasant when you finally exposed him.'

'It was.'

'You were shocked.'

'Horrified.'

Middlecheap decelerated again. He interlaced one set of fingers with the other on Wesley's blotter. His eyes were like two pale grey buttons. The forefinger of one hand bobbed lightly up and down on the plump hairless back of the other.

'When you kept an eye,' he said. 'Tell me, how did you go about it?'

'Very unscientifically, I'm afraid. I looked through his desk from time to time; went through his diary occasionally; but short of following him at lunchtimes and going through his pockets there was little I could do. I suggested to Mr. Quilter that he called in the Special Branch; which he had already done, although I didn't know that at the time.'

'They searched his house, you know,' Middlecheap confided. 'They could find nothing.'

'His wife did tell me that; at his funeral.'

'She told you nothing else? Nothing that might hint at – .' Middlecheap hunted around for an apt phrase. ' – his extra-mural activities, shall we say?'

'She was convinced he didn't engage in any.'

Middlecheap changed tack. He wanted to know about Lomax the man. The Lomax who had won the Military Cross in Crete in 1943. The Lomax who had rented the smart flat in Georgiadis Street in Athens, who gave discreet little dinner and drinking parties, who enjoyed young people about him.

'And these young people, they were mostly from the diplomatic set?'

'Almost entirely.'

'Of various nationalities?'

'Yes. Although he was ostensibly the Assistant Head of Chancery, he was in fact working for MI. He made a number of useful contacts.'

'Russians, for instance?'

'Yes. Several. I think he mentioned that on the tape we all heard at the preliminary to this enquiry. He made no bones about it.'

'And what were his politics? Did he ever say?'

'Agnostic.'

'He actually said that?'

'Frequently.'

Middlecheap smiled again, but without humour this time. 'And supposing it was suggested that he was an ardent Communist? That his political agnosticism might have been a cover for views of a more extreme kind?'

Tread softly, Coast told himself. Weigh this one.

'If it had been suggested to me, I would have dismissed it out of hand.'

'Is that the past tense you're employing, Mr. Coast; or the present.'

'I'm not sure.'

The two plump white hands, at rest now, were examined lengthily.

'So despite the fact that it was yourself who finally exposed Lomax, you still own to doubts of some kind? Is that it?'

'I've already told you, I'd known the man for nearly twenty years. Revealing him for what he was – if a traitor was what he was – gave me no sense of triumph. That's what I'm saying.'

'So even though he might have been a traitor, he still had some of your sympathy. – Oh, believe me, I can understand that. It's a perfectly reasonable reaction.'

'Yes,' agreed Coast. 'I did think along those lines.'

'Still?'

Coast shrugged. 'I'm not sure the evidence was completely damning. Even now.'

'Are you saying that that list you found in Lomax's briefcase had been put there inadvertently? – That's hardly likely, is it?'

'No, it isn't.'

'So what are you saying, Mr. Coast?'

Coast stubbed out his cigarette. 'It did occur to me that someone else might have put it there. At the time.'

'And did you have grounds for thinking that?'

'None at all.'

Middlecheap parted his hands and spread them a few inches apart. Well, the gesture said, we're on the same wavelength, what are we worrying about.

'Assume, shall we, that Lomax did hide that list in his briefcase. What was it worth in terms of intelligence gathering?'

'Of itself, nothing. But it was a means to an end.'

'How?'

'It would enable a Soviet surveillance-vessel to listen out on exactly the right frequencies at exactly the right time. It wouldn't miss a word.'

Lunchtime came and went and Middlecheap neither rubbed his hands together nor glanced at his watch. Many of his questions seemed to have little point to them, although he hung upon every answer as though it mattered. Some questions were repeats of earlier ones re-phrased and sharpened up so that they became more penetrating and required a response in more detail. And Coast, by degrees, began to give more details. He began to withdraw from his previously held position of Lomax's loyal friend, and to exhibit doubts on his own account. Yes, he had known for many years that Lomax was an alcoholic, that of late Lomax had been teetering on a financial knife-edge; and that Lomax's disinterest in matters political might have been only a front for something more ideological. That was just possible.

'He mostly worked alone, I believe.'

'Understandable,' said Coast. 'He was the only member of the department who spoke Greek and Turkish.'

'So he had, as it were, made a corner for himself.'

'Yes. Looked at that way. I suppose he had.'

'A very convenient position that would be; don't you agree? Working alone, relatively unsupervised, coming and going more or less as he pleased, access to information about a particularly sensitive zone of NATO operations.'

Middlecheap had the helm. And Coast knew that all he had to do was to make an occasional trim of the sails.

Late on a sunny summer evening, the view from St. James's Park towards Whitehall is again transformed. The kingdom is tinted a mellow gold, its turrets and finials glitter, and its foreground of lovely trees become more sharply and luminously defined. The ducks on the lake drift idly, rather than paddle, and from time to time their eyes blink sleepily. It is the end of their day too.

Quilter's cigarette hissed to extinction in the water and he lit another.

'We bloody killed him, David, you know that don't you? We all drummed up a bloody conspiracy.'

'That's not what Middlecheap said.'

Quilter spat smoke angrily as he shot Tribe a bitter glance along his shoulder.

'Near enough, by God. We've been had David. Somewhere along the bloody line we've all been taken for a ride. You, me, Mingay, the whole damned heap of us.'

A light breeze rippled the leaves of the distant trees. Further along the bridge, just out of earshot, Fairhazel was leaning on the rail and apparently doing little more than aimlessly watching his own reflection in the water.

'David, if it's anyone else ... We're running out of time. Where the hell do we start?'

'We don't start, Tony. We continue where we left off. We take Middlecheap's private opinion and add it to Charlie Fairhazel's. We'll set the bugger up and hoist him on his own bloody petard.'

'But all Middlecheap suggested was that the man seemed just a little too eager to co-operate, for God's sake.'

'And that he followed wherever Middlecheap chose to lead him,' added Tribe more trenchantly.

Quilter inhaled deeply on his cigarette.

'Private opinion, David. Mingay wants facts.'

'He didn't exactly want facts about Lomax, did he,' retorted Tribe, with quiet vehemence. 'He wanted a scalp.'

'And now he concedes he made an error of judgement.'

'Christ,' said Tribe. 'Is that what he calls it? – Perhaps he should try telling poor Mrs. Lomax that.'

Quilter made no reply.

Footsteps sounded on the deck of the bridge. A small, prissy woman in a tartan cape was walking her goggle-eyed pekingese dog to which she bore more than a passing resemblance. Tribe waited until she had gone out of earshot, then leaned further forward over the guard-rail.

'Will you join us, please, Charlie,' he called softly.

Fairhazel straightened himself and ambled along the bridge towards them.

'Yes, Colonel?'

'Coast, Charlie. What you think and what you know.'

Fairhazel turned in beside them and folded his arms on the rail. He briefly stretched the outer corners of his mouth. Another evening breeze sent a pattern of ripples across the lake.

'Well, sir, he's a crafty bugger. Definitely on the dodgy side.'

'And what on earth does that mean?' Quilter asked testily.

'We've been into his flat, Mr. Quilter. Tailed him a couple of times, like we did all the others. Mr. Coast did seem to stand out, you might say.'

'Oh, for God's sake,' said Quilter; but then instantly bit that back whence it came. 'Forgive me, Mr. Fairhazel. I'm sorry. – It's just that I've known the man for years.'

'And that's just what Coast said about Lomax, isn't it?' Tribe reminded them pointedly. 'Go on, Charlie.'

'I sent Prebble down to read Coast's electricity meter and chat up his cleaner. – She says she hardly ever sees him. He puts her cash under an ashtray on the kitchen-table every

Friday, and if he wants her to do anything particularly, he leaves her a note. And she does the same. He's a very tidy man, she says. – And drinks like a fish. Two to three bottles a week. Scotch. He dumps the empties in the bin in the kitchen. Naturally, my lad couldn't take the place apart, but he did spin her a yarn about his brother hoping to move into that particular block. So the good lady took him on a guided tour.'

'And he found something?'

'No, Mr. Quilter, not exactly. – But he noticed a few things. For instance, the wardrobe door was locked and the key wasn't in it. Unusual that, for a man who lives on his own.'

'Perhaps he's scared of burglars.'

'Hardly, sir. Prebble reckons he could have sprung the door with a table-knife. He's probably more interested in just keeping the cleaner from looking in there. He's got a glass-doored bookcase in his lounge. That's kept locked as well, probably for exactly the same reason. Again, there was no sign of a key – all cheap books too. Paperbacks mostly. Nothing of any value at all. Bottle of Scotch on the sideboard. Safeway's price-tag on it. Three-quarters empty – and the cleaner said he'd only started on it the day before. So he's definitely a boozer.'

'But that's still scarcely evidence,' ventured Quilter. His cigarette followed the last one over the rail, but this time he did not light another.

'No, sir, it isn't,' agreed Fairhazel equably. 'But we set up an intermittent tailing operation when all this business started. Mr. Fanning, Mr. Toler, Mr. Templeton – even yourself, Mr. Quilter. And the only one to turn up trumps was Mr. Coast.'

A double footfall resounded on the bridge. A young couple this time, moony-gazed and with arms about each other's waists. The girl laughed softly and offered up her face. They paused, kissed, dawdled slowly on again. The footfalls receded, then were gone.

'Coast gave Prebble the slip. Prebble managed to keep in touch with him for about half-an-hour – a bus, a taxi, another bus – that bus looked like a back-track, by the way. Then Coast hopped on the Tube at Camden Town – and hopped off again at Belsize Park – while the doors were closing; as if he'd suddenly remembered he'd gone past his station.'

'Perhaps he had,' ventured Quilter.

'No, Mr. Quilter,' said Fairhazel, with an air of finality. 'If that man's anything at all, he's a professional. Bet your life.'

'Then why the hell didn't you pursue it?' asked Quilter.

'Because it wasn't evidence, Mr. Quilter; and you'd pointed us at Mr. Lomax. – Then that piece of paper turned up in Lomax's briefcase and Mr. Mingay called us off altogether.'

There was a moment of silence.

'How soon can the investigation be re-activated?' asked Quilter suddenly. 'How soon?'

'As soon as Mingay gives us the go-ahead,' replied Tribe.

'Then see him, David. And quickly. Please.'

They came off the bridge in the pearly dusk. A huge white dog, moving silently, like a ghost, bounded across the grass in front of them, skidded to a stop and closed its teeth about a yellow rubber ball. It quickly turned about and loped back in silence to its master.

'You're keeping an eye on the Daily Telegraph, of course.'

'Yes,' replied Quilter. 'Thank God, Peterson hasn't been in touch with him yet.'

'And bait,' said Tribe. 'We need bait. Tempt his taste-buds with an irresistible tit-bit or two.'

'Consider it done,' said Quilter. 'But let's just hope to God we're right this time, eh?'

'Perhaps we ought to emulate old Noll Cromwell,' suggested Tribe drily, after a few paces. 'And hope that God knows which side he's actually on. What?'

And Quilter nodded humourlessly as they stepped out under the lamplights of Birdcage Walk.

'Yes, David,' he said. 'Quite.'

Twelve

And now there was another problem, not as yet too serious, but which might soon be, another irritation from an entirely different direction. Katerina Lomax had taken legal advice about the cessation of Lomax's salary.

' – And there's also the question of his pension. Even our own lawyers can't decide what the legal position is until Middlecheap finishes that damned report. If it comes out the wrong way she can make a devil of a lot of noise. It could all go public. D'you see?'

'So Mingay slaps down a D-notice.'

'Come on, Jocelyn,' snapped Quilter. 'You know better than that. Getting D-notices these days is damned near impossible.' He had been slowly pacing, a few steps this way, a few steps that way. Now he dropped into his chair as he finally came to the point of calling Coast along here at this late hour of a Friday afternoon.

'Mingay thinks we ought to sound her out. Nothing official; a friendly visit. You know the form.'

'*I* know the form?'

Quilter had the grace to glance down for a moment.

'It was Mingay's idea,' he said. 'I offered to go myself. But I hardly know the woman; and I might seem like an *eminence grise* – if you see what I mean.'

Lomax's house was in Purley, small, mock-Tudor, gabled, detached, with a garage built on to one side, the sort of place that speculative builders threw up in the days between the wars. He parked the Volvo by the kerb a few doors further along the avenue. He should have rung to warn Katerina of his coming, but he had not. Forewarned, he had decided, was forarmed. Catching her by surprise would throw her off balance. It would be bad enough facing her in any case, let alone with a battery of prepared questions in her hand.

The garden badly needed weeding, he noticed that particularly; and the hedge cutting. As the gravel of the drive crunched under his feet he thought he saw a net curtain move at the downstairs bay-window. A yellow Citroën estate-car stood in the garage, a dent still in its near-side front wing.

When he thumbed the door-bell, a double chime sounded; and the second one was still echoing when Katerina Lomax opened the door, so he had not imagined the stir of the net curtain. Part surprised, part pleased to see him.

She raised her face as they shook hands, and he kissed her cheek.

'How lovely to see you, Jocelyn,' she said, holding on to his hand the way she had done that morning at the cemetery. 'Quite marvellous. Such a surprise. Do come in. Please.'

He handed over the bunch of carnations he had stopped to buy outside a hospital on the way through from Streatham.

'So kind of you, Jocelyn. Thank you. So much.' She captured his hand again with her free one as she hugged the flowers close to herself. 'I am so glad you have come. Really. For weeks I have been going mad here on my own. Talking to myself; you know?'

'Spur of the moment,' he said. 'If it's inconvenient, you've only got to say.'

'No,' she said. 'Nonsense. Come. I was just making a cup of tea – Eric and I always had a cup of tea at this time on a Sunday afternoon.' She smiled thinly. 'I have become thoroughly English, you see.'

She showed him into the lounge, then went on through to the kitchen. He heard the clatter of crockery as she got out a cup and saucer for him.

Lomax was everywhere. A picture of him on the sideboard showed him as a cherubically faced youth in army uniform during the war. On the mantelshelf was another, with Katerina this time, taken years later amidst the ruins of the Acropolis. Only after he had left the house was he to remember that he had, in fact, taken that particular snapshot himself, and that Frances had a similar photograph, taken only a minute or two later, with himself on the other side of Katerina. One of the two chintzy armchairs was scarcely worn, the other bagged out with heavy use; that would have been Lomax's. A half-dozen Sunday newspapers lay on the coffee-table, folded much as they had come from the newsagent's, clearly unread, as if she no longer wanted them but had forgotten to cancel them.

She came in with tea things on a brass-handled tray, and nudged the stack of newspapers to one side with it as she set it down.

When she asked him to sit down, he sat, without thinking, in Lomax's chair.

'This isn't an official visit, is it, Jocelyn?' she asked, a fingertip on the lid of the teapot to stay it as she poured.

'Good Heavens, no,' he said. 'I suddenly felt I ought to come and see you. Ergo: I came.'

'Good,' she said. 'I am glad. – Every day, I have been half-expecting your Mr. Quilter or your Mr. Mingay to call. – But somehow I do not think they dare.'

She topped up the cups with milk, then brought his over to him with the sugar bowl.

'How are you?' she said. 'I'm so sorry, I forgot to ask.'

'Well,' he said. He helped himself to a single cube and dropped it into his cup. 'But more importantly, how are you? Managing?'

She shrugged as she turned away.

'Oh, yes,' she said. 'Just. Just managing.'

'It takes time,' he said. 'Or so they tell us.'

'Yes,' she said, giving him another of the smiles that weren't quite. 'So they tell us.' She sat carefully, balancing her cup as she primly adjusted her skirt over her knees. 'But frankly, Jocelyn, I have not reached the stage where I can believe that yet. You know?'

Behind her brittle gaiety, although not far behind, he could sense the bitterness in her. It pricked at his nerves more than he had thought it would. The bagged out armchair had a sag in the seat and it required a conscious effort not to slide back deeper into it.

Talk gradually drifted into the old times. He could handle that. Lomax figured prominently, but distantly, a manageable spectre.

It was an hour or more before he led her subtly into the subject of her finances. She had made another pot of tea and brought in a silver-handled plate with a small pile of biscuits on it.

'I saw the car on the way in,' he said, casually. 'Going all right, is it?'

'Yes,' she said. 'Although I'm still waiting for the insurance company to settle the claim Eric put in about one of the front wings.'

'Yes,' he said, taking his third cup of tea from her. 'Eric told me about that. – Expensive business, these days, panel-beating.'

'They want seventy pounds. They told me I could have a whole new wing for a hundred, but the insurance company won't agree.'

'Look, Kat,' he began hesitantly. 'I meant what I said at Eric's funeral; anything I can do.'

She seemed not to understand. She frowned at him over the rim of her cup.

'Eric did tell me things were tight,' he explained. ' – If I can help in that direction, I'd be only too glad. – I mean that.'

She protested at once, leaping, as it were, to Lomax's defence as a provider. But it was not a strong defence. It was all right, she told him. There had been two insurance policies, both of which she had been paid within a week of Lomax's funeral. They would be enough.

'Enough to tide you over, then?'

No, they would not, at least for very long. She didn't say so but he could tell by the way she looked at him.

'The truth, Kat,' he urged, leaning forward towards her. 'Come on. Tell me honestly.'

'No,' she admitted at last, grudgingly. 'They will only be enough to settle the debts we had. – Eric was not good with money. – We were always behind. – Oh, small things; you know? The bills; gas, electricity, the rates, the telephone, the car tax; all the bills that are nothing when they come one at a time, but once they are allowed to accumulate – oh, you know, one can never quite catch up. You know how Eric was ... never do today what you may also be able to put off again tomorrow.' Then she put out a hand, a staying gesture. ' – No. I do not mean that. Really. Not the way it sounds. He was kind – and only sometimes a little foolish.' She shrugged. 'And who is not, sometimes.'

That delivered, she looked wistfully down into her cup.

'So what's the extent of your problem?' he asked. 'Come along, Kat, if you can't tell me, who can you tell, for Heaven's sake?'

She took a while to answer. She stirred what remained of the tea in her cup.

'About eleven hundred pounds, Jocelyn,' she replied at last. She shrugged again, only this time she made of it an expression of hopelessness. 'Oh, he was mad. He bought a greenhouse on hire-purchase – to give him something to do when he retired – and there are four hundred pounds still owing on that wretched car – that thing – .' She pointed at the television-set. 'Fifty pounds still on that. All little things.'

'The insurance money won't cover the debts, then? Nowhere near?'

She slowly shook her head.

'No.'

'So you weren't telling me the truth just now?'

Her head continued to shake.

'No, Jocelyn. They were small policies. All the big ones he had – how do you say?'

'Surrendered?'

'Yes. Surrendered.' One by one. Over the years. To buy things. To pay debts, bills. This stupid thing – a platinum-set diamond ring, bought for her on their thirtieth wedding anniversary – because her original engagement-ring had been such a poor thing – she had had it valued – last week in Croydon. The man in the shop had offered her eight hundred pounds for it, thinking she wanted to sell it.

'Eric said – oh, I did not know what it had cost him – except that it was more than we could afford – it's an investment, old girl. Just an investment. Investment!' Her voice rose on a note part anger, part derisory. 'What is an investment that you cannot realise? – Oh, Jocelyn – .'

He felt his skin shrinking with embarrassment, or perhaps it was conscience; whatever it was, it made him feel distinctly ill at ease.

When he offered her some financial assistance – call it a loan, he told her, long term, no interest – it was some time before he eventually persuaded her to accept it. He used his own cheque-book. On Monday he would be reimbursed out of the Section's slush fund, used in the main to bribe, procure or hush as the occasions arose. Mingay had authorised any amount up to a thousand pounds. In the event she accepted, with much reluctance, his cheque for six hundred pounds. She would pay him back when she received the money outstanding to Lomax, although she was not sure when that was going to be. She had seen a solicitor who had advised her to take the matter to court if the Treasury dragged its feet for very much longer.

'Is that wise?' he asked her.

'Why *shouldn't* I grind their noses in it,' she said. 'Mr. Mingay and Mr. Quilter, they killed Eric – they did, Jocelyn,' she insisted when she thought he was going to deny it. 'Oh, no, not with a knife or a gun. That they would not have the courage to do. But they did kill him, Jocelyn. The same way as a witch-doctor kills by pointing the bone. *They pointed the bone, Jocelyn.*'

'Revenge, Kat?' he said. 'Is that what you're after?'

'Oh, I don't know,' she replied. 'Yes. Perhaps I do. I also want people to know.'

'And what happens if the press wants a better story?'

She did not understand.

'How do you mean?'

'Look,' he explained patiently. 'I can't officially tell you of the sort of work Eric was doing – and the press isn't going to find out either; but they'll guess, Kat, the way you've guessed. And if I'm right, the boys from Fleet Street will have a field-day. – They could pillory him, Kat, and there's no one in the world, except you, who could possibly fight back for him, – I certainly couldn't. Do you follow?'

'Are you warning me off, Jocelyn; is that it?'

'Of course I'm not. – I'm cautioning good sense. If the enquiry decides that Eric wasn't guilty, and you've got court-proceedings in the pipe-line ... ' He left the rest unspoken for her imagination to deal with.

'There's no hurry,' he said. 'But if I were you, I'd certainly think about it.'

'What did she say?' asked Quilter, early on the Monday morning.

'Nothing,' replied Coast. 'We don't have to worry about her.'

Thirteen

Quilter came away from the tipple-cabinet with two brimming glasses.

'The clouds seem to be lifting,' he said. 'Middlecheap hopes he'll have his report finished by the end of next week. With any luck we may have avoided even a minor scandal.' He leaned across the desk with one glass and stood the other on his blotter. It was rare to see him in waistcoat and shirtsleeves and looking this relaxed. When he sat down, his fingertips went beneath his chin in his usual attitude of prayerful contemplation. 'To come to the point; how busy are you?'

'Only middling.' Wesley was still on leave, Templeton and Fanning had just started theirs. 'I'm keeping a watching-brief on the job Toler's doing, and working on that report you wanted about the new security arrangements.'

'And nothing else in the pipeline? Nothing you can't hand over to Toler or someone?'

'If I do that,' he replied jokily, 'I won't have any dam' work at all.'

'Precisely,' said Quilter. There followed a moment more of contemplation; then Quilter stirred himself to his feet and fished his safe-key out of his waistcoat. He went to the wall-safe beside the drink-cabinet, gave the dial a few twists in either direction, then inserted the key. It was only a small shallow safe and the crudely-bound wad of papers he drew out of it all but filled it. When he turned and dumped the wad on the corner of his desk it was heavy enough to make the sherries ripple in their glasses. He closed the safe, then slipped the key back into his waistcoat pocket. The sherries rippled again as he dropped the document down in front of Coast.

'Grade One confidential, Jocelyn,' he said, lowering himself into his chair. 'A nine till four-thirty job. You collect it from me each morning and bring it back each afternoon. The conditions,' he added, 'Are Mingay's.'

Coast turned the tattered looking bundle to read the title, then picked it up in one hand and weighed it. It was difficult to affect disinterest.

'Feels like a few billion francs-worth of French Air-Budget,' he said.

'Exactly,' agreed Quilter.

'How the hell did we come by it?'

'Mingay did. Privately. Last week. He was made a present of it by a Right-Wing French Deputy who doesn't believe in the new socialism. It forecasts their possible requirements for the next five years.'

It was incredibly comprehensive. Typescripts, charts, graphs, computer print-outs, hierarchical diagrams, a few maps of proposed airfield and missile sites. It had all been Xeroxed, five or six hundred pages by the feel of it, a lot of it clumsily, the print on the skew here and there as if the operator had been in a hurry; which was likely in the circumstances. In terms of its commodity-value on the intelligence market it was undefiled gold. A month ago he could have passed it all across to Michael.

Quilter's fingers were back beneath his chin.

'It's been promised to Washington,' he said. 'But in the meantime, Mingay wants it winnowed. A comprehensive digest of everything you can find that might be of help to the Strategic Studies people. Xerox if you have to; but do it yourself. Nothing to be typed, and only we two know that it exists. To anyone else, it doesn't.'

'How long?'

Quilter's fingertips parted briefly, then came together again.

'A month,' he said. 'Then it has to go to Washington. It's

going to be a push, I realise that, but that's all the time we can spare, I'm afraid. I do apologise.'

'And I can't burn the midnight oil?'

'No,' said Quilter. 'Sorry.'

'And what about the security exercise?'

'Drop it,' said Quilter.

Back in the silence of his own office he lit a cigarette. With Wesley away on one side and Templeton on the other ... and Quilter had given him every excuse to lock his office door ... it was definitely a camera job, if only he dared to take the risk of smuggling one in and out. But he stopped at the thought. The shadow of Eric Lomax was still too close. Measure the risk, never take a chance. Luck does not exist. The first Michael had come up behind him in the Strand one lunch-time and touched his sleeve. I do beg your pardon, sir, but I'm sure we know each other, don't we? It could have been at Oxford. The summer of 'sixty. I think, I rarely forget a face. They had had a drink together, then strolled along the Embankment in the wintry sunshine, and Michael had reiterated all Nikky Borisenki's adjurations as if he had learned them by rote. But one more, confided over a hand-shake beneath the entrance canopy of the Embankment Underground station. Take no chances. *Nothing* is worth the risk of your exposure. Always remember that. There is no such thing as luck.

That was the evening Frances rang, her teeth sinking into his throat the moment he picked the receiver up.

'The small matter of a dress, Jocelyn.'

'Dress?'

'A dress for Susan. I'm not sure whether it was implied or promised, but whichever it was the child's expecting it.'

'Frances ... I'm deeply sorry.'

'You are taking her to this concert I suppose?'

'Yes, ... I'll put a cheque in the post first thing tomorrow.'

Her teeth relaxed their hold on his throat.

'Kat Lomax rang me yesterday.'

'Oh, yes?' He patted his pockets for cigarettes, but remembered he had left them in his jacket.

'I think you might have told me, Joss. At least I could have sent some flowers.'

'I had your name put on mine,' he said. 'And the children's.'

'Well thank you for that; but I still wish you'd told me. It was quite a shock hearing it from Kat; I couldn't think of anything to say.'

'It's been a hectic time,' he explained. 'You'll just have to believe that. Bad for all of us.'

'Yes,' she said. 'Yes. I can imagine.' Her voice had undergone a subtle change and lost its pithiness. She and Kat Lomax must have had a long and deedy conversation. She even knew of his promised good offices on Lomax's behalf at the enquiry.

'I hope you did speak for him, Jocelyn.'

'I did,' he said. And to ameliorate the pricklings of his conscience: 'There wasn't exactly a great deal of evidence. Nothing was proved either one way or the other.'

'Somebody set him up; that's what Eric told Katerina.'

A dentist's drill, shrieking on a raw nerve.

'It's possible,' he said. 'Remotely.'

'But what do you think, Joss? Privately. I mean, who would have?'

'Frances,' he said. 'I can't discuss it. You know how these things are.'

One of her silences, a weary one.

'Yes, Joss. I know exactly how these things are. You always were an impersonal bastard where other people were concerned, weren't you. Goodbye – and don't forget that cheque, will you?'

And before he could reply there was a click and the line was dead.

By ten o'clock the silence was screaming at him, and he switched on the television while he went into the kitchen to put a sandwich together and brew some coffee. The entire world seemed to be moving away from him. Michael had still not come up with anything about the Minaret business. Peterson had gone out of touch, and with a lot of the staff away the Section was like a tomb. He was in a vacuum, that was what it felt like.

When he returned to the lounge the pictures on the news were very much the same as last night's; and last week's come to that. The Arabs were still the terrorists, and the Israelis and the Americans the good guys. There had been another kidnapping in Italy; the trade talks in Geneva between the Russians and the Americans had broken down in disorder ...

His cup, rising to his mouth, did not reach it. According to Peterson, this was the Ides of March. When the talks finished, Minaret's defection was imminent.

He watched them come out of the conference building, the hardnosed Russian chief delegate accusing the Americans and the hardnosed American accusing the Russians. No. There would be no more talks. Not until next year, at the earliest. A body of Swiss police formed an arcade so that the delegates could get to their cars.

On Wednesday he lunched alone at his usual place in the Strand, pencilling in the answers to the Telegraph crossword while he ate his salad. On the way here he had telephoned Michael from the booth at Charing Cross station. The investigators at Centre were working flat out, but so far they had not come up with anything that could lead to Minaret.

'We're running out of time,' he told Michael. 'The crossing's imminent.'

'Do you think I don't know that,' Michael had retorted. 'I am as helpless as you are.'

He could usually complete the crossword in twenty minutes or less. Today his mind wouldn't run to it. He checked the personal-columns for the third time that day in case he had missed a message from Peterson; but he had not. Quilter had again chased him up about that this morning.

'Nothing, Jocelyn! Mingay intends to give him one more month; then we cease our subscriptions. If you hear from him, tell him that.'

The Embankment was hung with petrol fumes and the fine grey dust that the traffic flung up and left to float in the heat; and all the girls were high-heeled and short skirted and flaunting their tight little backsides, and trying to look as if they didn't sweat like everyone else on a day like this one.

If it was nothing else his office was cool, the Venetian-blinds closed, a swinging fan on the window ledge rhythmically blowing cool air at the nape of his neck. This morning he had written another two pages of Mingay's digest, and this afternoon one half of him seethed with impatience to share all this with Michael while the other half shook with trepidation at the thought. He had reached the chapter headed *Forces Aeriennes Strategique*, the nuclear arm of the French Air Force.

When his telephone rang it nine o'clock he leapt to it. Michael had promised to ring the moment he heard anything from Centre. I am so sorry, he was to say, I seem to have the wrong number. So sorry to have troubled you.

Only it wasn't Michael. It was Roma Peterson and it took him a moment to make the rush of adrenalin subside.

'Where are you?'

'Here.' A gurgle of syrupy laughter. '*A Londres.* – And you won't believe this, hon, but Gus has *sent* me. To see *you.* – Which means he's both blind *and* stupid and proves what I've been thinking for years.'

'When can I see you?'

'Gus did say it was urgent.'

'Well, then.' He smiled impatiently into the mouthpiece. 'Why waste time? Why not now?'

'Sounds fine.' She was staying at a small private hotel in Kensington; none of the larger hotels had been able to put her up at such short notice. And there was a smart little Chinese restaurant, a few doors along the street, where they could eat.

Eros leered down with tobacco-stained teeth and boozy

breath. A faint blue light from a neon sign further along the street sent a chill glow off the ceiling.

The sand was running all too quickly out of the glass. When she had taken her room-key out of her handbag in the lift on the way up to her room he had glimpsed the corner of a white envelope sticking up among her plethora of junk. Half an hour had elapsed since then. It was almost one o'clock. He needed the envelope, to get back to Steatham, to 'phone Michael. He had no idea what was in the envelope, but instinct told him Peterson would not have sent his wife over at such short notice without good reason. And the best reason at the moment was Minaret's defection.

Sitting up beside him, her flesh glowed pinkly as she drew on her cigarette. She exhaled noisily.

'Not one of your better performances,' she said, reaching out to switch on the lamp beside the bed. 'If I thought about it, I'd say you had another source of supply.'

He made no answer. Even in the dark her hot greedy body had failed to excite him.

A minute or two passed in silence. The lift rose and its doors clattered noisily open, then footsteps passed by in the passage. Silence fell again.

'Will I be seeing you tomorrow?'

Long accustomed to lies on the grand scale, the small ones tripped off his tongue without his thinking about them.

'I'm flying up to Scotland,' he said.

'For how long?'

'Three or four days; I'm not sure yet.'

She didn't so much exhale smoke as spit it out.

'You're kidding,' she said. 'You mean I've come over here – and you're flying off somewhere. God! I don't believe it!'

Her mood stayed and there was nothing he felt like doing about it. After tonight she was surplus to requirements. He would no longer need her, nor Peterson for that matter.

He dressed while she stormed off angrily to the bathroom. She came back tugging tight the sash of a towelling-robe about her middle. With her back to him, she took a packet of cigarettes out of her handbag on the dressing-table and lit one.

'You didn't mention Scotland on the 'phone,' she said. 'Why not?'

'Because I wasn't aware then that I was going.'

'How bloody convenient,' she said, turning to face him as he buttoned his shirt. 'You sound exactly like Gus. You know that? You're all the dam' same.'

'Gus only read out those telex numbers to you?' he asked, businesslike, ignoring her comments. 'There was no other message?'

'No,' she said. 'I told you.'

She watched impatiently while he tied his shoelaces.

'If you're still here on Monday evening, give me a ring.'

'Don't worry,' she said. 'I won't be.'

He shrugged, and reached for his jacket. 'Up to you,' he said.

She made no reply. In the light of the lamp, her mouth was set in a grim, hard line. She twisted out her cigarette in the ashtray, then dipped into her handbag for the white envelope and thrust it out at him.

'And you'll want this,' she said.

'You're sure there was no other message? I mean, absolutely sure?'

'Christ, I'm going mad. Yes. I keep telling you.'

He tucked the envelope into the inside pocket of his jacket.

'And you're sure about the numbers?' he said. 'You didn't miss any?'

'Look, sport,' she said angrily, closing a few inches and staring up at him, 'When he read those out to me it was four o'clock in the goddam' morning. If I did make a mistake then frankly I don't give a fuck. Now just go, will you.'

He went to peck at her cheek, but she warded him off and jerked her face away. He backed a pace, and screwed a smile into position.

'If you change your mind,' he said. 'Ring me on Monday.'

She padded stiffly past him to the door and held it open.

'You're pushing your luck, Jocelyn,' she said. 'You've got what you came for. Now, out!'

In the passage, he turned to make some placatory comment; but the door was already closing in his face.

He hurried back to where he had parked the car, in a side-street off Brompton Road, and as soon as he was settled in switched on the courtesy-light and ran a finger under the flap of the envelope. In the dim light he unfolded the single sheet of paper it contained. Pencilled untidily on it was a single vertical row of nine-figure numbers that Peterson had read to her over the telephone from Lubeck. He stuffed the paper back into the envelope and the envelope into his jacket.

He drove quickly through the empty streets. At two o'clock he was unlocking the door to the flat, and by five past was sitting on the settee with the pencilled list and a notepad on his knee, and a Paris street-guide, opened at the index pages, on the cushion beside him. The code he and Peterson had concocted between them was crudely simple. The first number in the row of what Roma Peterson had been told were telex addresses, represented the relevant page of the index, the next figure the first, second or third column of that page. Having established those all he had to do was write down the first letter that appeared at the head of that column, then go to the next pair of numbers on the list, and so on. It was ponderous, but as codes went it was very nearly unbreakable without the street guide.

The first word he decoded was *Sunday*. The next two figures were preceded by a zero, so they were figures as they stood – 28. The coming Sunday was the 28th of July.

The next word meant nothing to him. *Colgen*. He spent a moment checking that back. He had transcribed it correctly. If there was a mistake it had been generated at Peterson's end. Two letters on their own. N A. Initials, perhaps. He moved on quickly; the numbers; the guide; another letter added to the pad. He wrote six of them with gathering premonition, and the last three he did not even bother to commit to paper.

Nikky Borisenko was a Colonel-General now.

And about to defect.

Pfft! Like that.

Fourteen

A crisis situation, and unbelievably they had sent the girl.

They boarded the first incoming train and stood impersonally back to back as far as St. James's Park.

At street level the girl waited at the kerb for a taxi while Coast went ahead on foot. The taxi caught him up half-way along Tothill Street. He boarded it almost before it had stopped, and slid shut the privacy-window behind the driver's head, all but tumbling into the seat beside the girl as the taxi shot forward.

'I telephoned for a meet with Michael. Where is he?'

'He is busy,' the girl said. 'He will meet you at the Hampstead place this evening. Any time.'

'There isn't any bloody time,' he retorted angrily. 'Tell Michael I know who Minaret is.'

'We do also,' said the girl, for the first time showing some sort of emotion. 'It is Colonel-General Borisenko.'

He felt a surge of relief.

'So you've managed to stop him.'

The girl looked bitterly along her shoulder at him.

'On the contrary. He has gone.'

'You mean you've let it happen, for Christ's sake?'

'We could not stop it,' the girl said. 'They were looking in the wrong place. They thought they were looking for a captain or a major – or at most a colonel. But a Colonel-General – .' Her eyes brimmed with disgust behind her spectacles at this failure of the masters to safeguard the servants'-hall. Loyalty can only be stretched so far, the eyes said, even among Russians, and for that moment she and

Coast were closer comrades than any two Englishmen or any two Russians anywhere else in the world. ' – A Colonel-General – one rank higher than that and he would report directly to the Praesidium. It is incredible.'

The taxi, stopped at traffic lights, moved forward into Parliament Square. Up on the left was the window of the room in which he had first met Middlecheap.

'Borisenko knows me,' he said. 'He recruited me.'

Never before had he uttered the name aloud. It had been his closest secret, never to be spoken to anyone, like the name of God to the old Jews.

'He was a big man in the KGB,' the girl said. 'It will be bad for all of us.'

'But me he can identify. You're all right. You can catch the first bloody Aeroflot back to Moscow.'

'We always look after our own people. We shall get you out.'

'So I keep hearing.'

The taxi stopped beside the Cenotaph and joined the queue waiting to enter Trafalgar Square.

'Borisenko will be in Mildenheim sometime early on Sunday morning.'

She glanced sharply at him.

'For sure?'

'For absolutely bloody sure. Michael knows the rest. Eight o'clock in the town square. He's being picked up there by the CIA. – Just tell Michael not to bungle it.'

The taxi turned into Trafalgar Square and circled it, and stopped again at the traffic-lights at the corner of the National Gallery and St. Martin's Place. As Coast reached for the door-handle, the girl gripped his wrist.

'When shall Michael expect you?'

'Eight,' he said. 'As near as I can make it.'

He got down from the taxi and swung the door shut. It turned left up Charing Cross Road and went from sight.

He let himself be absorbed into the crowd crossing the street and walking down past the steps of St. Martins towards the Strand and Whitehall. If he sensed anything at all, it was an even greater awareness of his isolation, that he was different from all who surrounded him, the chattering office-girls, the umbrella swingers. He walked apart, seeing nothing, his ears full of the tramp of marching feet. When they all crossed the Strand, at the green light, so did he and let them suck him on down into Whitehall.

The brief display of his pass in the foyer.

'Good morning, Sam.'

' 'Morning, sir.'

Everything as normal. Up in the lift, all the faces familiar, Franklin complaining about his new income-tax assessment and Heatherington making sure that the knot of his necktie was properly centred between the wings of his collar for morning parade, Goldring looking like every schoolboy's dream up to her chin and an iceberg above it.

And then the parting of the ways, the ritual unlocking of office doors, each of them entering their compartments like so many battery hens.

Only then did he loose his breath, his back to his closed door, private at last and invisible. Nikky Borisenko, the erstwhile whipper in of traitors was a traitor now himself. He had gone from his desk in Dzerzhinski Square and no one knew where he was. Pfft! Like that.

Michael's sartorial schizophrenia was temporarily abated. He was in a middle-management grey suit, a matching tie, polished black shoes.

'We thought he was on leave,' he said, of Borisenko. 'But when his apartment was checked last night, his janitor said that he had not seen him in two days.'

And they had suspected nothing at all. Borisenko was a KGB staff-officer. Nobody dared to investigate anybody that high up in the KGB hierarchy. Now there was a tumult going on in the Square and everybody was accusing everybody else of lack of foresight.

Michael lit another of his cardboard-tubed cigarettes. A cut-glass ashtray beside him was littered with the stubs of them.

'He'll be in East Germany,' said Coast.

'So are fifteen million other people,' replied Michael testily.

'So look for him.'

'How? – When hardly anybody knows what he looks like.'

'Rubbish,' Coast retorted. 'Photos. Circulate them. The press; television.'

'There are no photographs,' said Michael. Today he was not dispassionate. The hand that lifted his cigarettes to his mouth had a nervous shake to it and his pale moist eyes shifted hither and thither. 'There are no photographs.'

There were no photographs anywhere, not in the Square, not in his apartment. All his files had disappeared, thirty years'-worth of them, even the duplicate set from the underground archives, deep under the Ural mountains. There were two copies also of his dossier on computer-tapes, but when they had been run through the machines they were both found to have been wiped clean. Colonel-General Nicholas Alexeivitch Borisenko might never have been.

'Then get the people who know him into East Germany. Sniff him out. You've got the resources, for God's sake.'

Michael had risen from his armchair and gone to stand looking down into the empty fireplace.

'Impossible,' he said. 'You say here, who guards the guards. In Moscow it was Borisenko. Only a dozen people at most knew who he was and what he was. And what could they do? Drag through every town in East Germany. I tell you, we are helpless.' His turned abruptly. 'It is even possible that he could be in West Germany by now. He will have to be taken care of in this Mildenheim place.'

'Then get someone who can recognise him into Mildenheim. Before eight o'clock on Sunday morning.'

He had always though of the KGB as a vast and efficient machine to which nothing was impossible; and here he was practically having to spell it out for them.

'We have an operator in Paris. A man we call Dennikin. He could be in Mildenheim by tomorrow evening.'

'Then you haven't got a problem.'

Michael gave a hunch to his shoulders.

'Only one,' he said. 'Dennikin is a reliable assassin; but he does not know Borisenko.'

There was silence.

'So you get someone into Mildenheim who does. Somebody who can identify the bastard.'

'It is a question of time.'

'I'd say it was more a question of organisation.'

'Time,' Michael insisted. 'We have only thirty-six hours. Less.' His gaze had stopped shifting about and now he was staring fixedly across at where Coast sat. There was about him the air of a man who had spent a long time coming to the nub of the matter, but now that he had arrived there had still a certain reluctance to put it into words. 'There is, of course, you. You told Litvinova this morning that Borisenko recruited you. Personally.'

Coast let out a harsh dry sound that wasn't quite a laugh.

'Twenty-odd years ago ... I might not recognise him. What happens then?'

'But you would recognise this man Peterson, would you not?'

Michael's voice had dropped to a tone of quiet persuasion.

'And you do have a vested interest,' he said.

It was plain that the matter was already arranged. They had probably spent all day planning it in one of the back rooms of the big house in Kensington Palace Gardens.

Michael took the two paces back to the settee, and sat this time at the end closest to Coast's armchair, so that they were almost knee to knee.

'You could do it easily,' he said. 'You could fly out tomorrow evening; fly back Sunday afternoon. It is a weekend. You would not be missed.'

'And if I'm in Germany at the time when Borisenko gets wiped out, they'll put two and two together. I'd be finished.'

'Use your emergency passport.'

'I've used it once already. It's too risky.'

'Use it. We can have a new one for you within a week. New papers. Everything.'

Michael's hand lay on Coast's knee. His grip tightened.

'You must,' he said. 'It is the only way.'

Coast's earlier guess was soon confirmed. The assassin Dennikin was already on his way by car from Paris. He had left at noon that day and would be in Mildenheim on Saturday evening. He would be travelling in a yellow Citroen estate. His Swedish passport was in the name of Bent Soderstrom. In Mildenheim there was one hotel and two *pensions*. Coast was to book into one as Mr. Tavistock, and stay put until his old business colleague, Soderstrom, came looking for him. There had been no time to make more sophisticated arrangements, but Dennikin would know what to do and any details could be shaped and trimmed at the meeting.

'So it's a *fait accompli*.'

'You can refuse to go.'

'It seems I bloody well have to go. – But when it comes to the kill, I'm out. I don't want to be involved.'

'You will not be. Dennikin is a professional.'

'And just Borisenko. Nothing happens to Peterson.'

'That I cannot say. It will have to be discussed with Dennikin.' Michael's hand slid away from Coast's knee. 'One cannot always choose who is a casualty in a war. – And you can imagine what your standing will be in Moscow if this matter is successfully concluded. The whole of the intelligence organisation of the Warsaw Pact could be given away by Borisenko to the people in the West. It would take us years to recover from such a blow. You would have stopped that happening.'

Air tickets would be at Coast's flat before he left for Whitehall in the morning. A late evening flight would be booked for him, and a room at the Adler in Hamburg. Mobility was essential. He should hire a car, but in Hamburg, not in Mildenheim. In Mildenheim his profile had to be kept low. He was to spend all of Saturday working out the lie of the land, so that he and Dennikin could make their eventual exits without a hitch.

' – And money.' Michael reached for his attaché-case further along the settee. He opened it and took out, as he had done the last time, a thick wad of mixed, used, English and German banknotes. Two hundred pounds, and three thousand Deutschmarks.

'I'll take the Deutschmarks.'

Michael stripped them away and tossed the sterling-notes back into his case then watched impassively as Coast divided the wad in two and distributed them between the two inside pockets of his jacket.

'Can you think of anything else you will need?'

'Only Dennikin.'

'Dennikin,' said Michael, 'will be there. I promise you.'

On Friday morning, very early, the airline tickets were lying on his doormat.

He caught an earlier train than usual to Victoria so that he could leave his overnight bag in the left luggage office. He intended to travel light, a spare shirt, pyjamas, shaver, a towel. His fake passport was wedged in under the stiffening-board at the bottom of the bag.

He was in his office well before nine, and collected Mingay's treasure-trove from Quilter soon after half-past. For the third day running his morning was undisturbed, and so was most of the afternoon, until Quilter came in soon after four o'clock. He looked decidedly out of sorts.

'Middlecheap has sent his report in to Mingay,' he said. 'If Lomax had appeared in court we wouldn't have had a case.'

'He warned us of that in the beginning.'

'Well, now we know for sure,' said Quilter. 'And Mingay's toying with the idea of bringing the Special Branch back in.'

'And will he?'

Quilter fumbled inside his jacket for his cigarette-case. 'I've told him,' he said. 'It's far too late. The tracks have been too heavily trodden over.'

He stayed for a few minutes. Coast pumped him for more news of Middlecheap's report, but either he knew no more than he had said or Mingay had told him to keep quiet about it. He went back to his own office, after a blow by blow account of what he intended to do in his garden if the weather held, still smoking the same cigarette.

The weather did not hold. By six o'clock it was raining. Coast took a taxi to the top end of Baker Street, the Tube to Edgware Road, where he had a meal in a snack-bar, another Tube to Gloucester Road, and finally a taxi to Victoria Station. It was by then half-past seven and the rush-hour was more or less over. He exchanged his briefcase for his overnight bag in the left-luggage office, and in the washroom, behind a bolted toilet door, he carried out the few necessary changes to turn himself into Mr. Tavistock.

That done, he hurried out into the forecourt and joined the queue for the taxis.

He rented a car from a garage in St. Pauli early on Saturday morning, and once again the Tavistock credentials passed muster.

'For how long?'

'Until tomorrow. Mid-day.' Although the car, an Escort estate, would be back here well before then. His flight out of Hamburg left at eleven-thirty tomorrow morning.

The girl who was dealing with him held back a wing of bleached hair as she copied the details of Tavistock's driving-licence and passport on to her pad of forms.

'Here please. – And here.'

He scribbled Tavistock's signature twice where she had pencilled crosses, then passed over four hundred marks in exchange for the car keys and his documents.

By nine o'clock, Hamburg lay well behind him and he was on the road to Mildenheim. It was a fine morning, and once out of the city a quieter mind than his might have noted the soft greens and golds of the countryside. But his was not a quiet mind. Middlecheap had put in his findings and Mingay was considering calling back the Special Branch and sometime today – or certainly tomorrow morning – Nicholas Borisenko, erstwhile field man and latterly a Centre mandarin was going to show his face in the West. It was like watching a glass fall to a concrete floor and being powerless to catch it.

The description of Dennikin that Michael had given him was vague. Dennikin was of medium height, medium build, dark. There had been no time to nominate a recognition-code of any kind, the newspaper under the arm, the flower in the buttonhole, the precisely scripted dialogue. Supposing the man who said he was Soderstrom was not Dennikin, but some other man of average height and average build with a swarthy complexion and dark hair? Someone the other side had introduced into the operation. Nothing was unlikely any more. And supposing Peterson was already in Mildenheim, had gone into panic and jumped the gun, holed up in the hotel or one of the *pensions* a day too early because his nerves had got the better of him and he was terrified of something going wrong?

These themes, and variations of them, and others, formed the train of his thoughts as he skirted Lubeck to the south round about ten o'clock and took the signposted route to Mildenheim. On this road, East Germany lay only a few kilometres to his left for most of the way, although he could not see the border. From time to time he glimpsed signs of life, a group of cottages, a tractor moving in a field, herds of cows, but he overtook no other vehicles and nothing overtook him. One private car passed him in the opposite direction, but that was all.

A length of road in a cutting, tightly curved beneath a canopy of trees, and where the trees abruptly ended a sign that read: Mildenheim. It was twenty past ten. He passed a few scattered cottages, a church, a filling station, then was taking the narrow sloping street into the village square. He drove slowly around it once, then pulled into the kerb in front of the village store. Not too obviously then he took in the view.

What was clearly the local inn-cum-hotel stood on the corner to the north east. It was white and clad with ivy, and on the pavement outside a couple of upended beer-barrels served as tables. In the diagonally opposite corner was another church. At least half the shop-fronts were boarded up, and half of the remainder were dilapidated. All that thrived were the general store and a double fronted place with its windows full of farming tools. And at the centre of the square was the granite obelisk of the war-memorial, where tomorrow morning Peterson was going to pick up Borisenko and speed him away to the safe-house in Lubeck if Dennikin botched it.

He bought a packet of cigarettes in the store and established the whereabouts of the two *pensions*. One was above the antique-shop in the street he had entered the square by, the other in the lane beside the church. Both had vacancies, so far as the storekeeper knew, as had the *gasthof* opposite. It had been a bad year for tourists. The economic depression. Even the Americans no longer came in any number with their cameras and field-glasses to look at the border the way they used to. Before the war, Mildenheim was a market centre, prosperous – and for a few years afterwards the British army of occupation had maintained a camp a few kilometres south, on the heath between here and Kaiserstadt, and that had brought business in to the local shopkeepers. But now the place was dying on its feet. All the young people were gone, most of them to the bright lights of Hamburg where the money was, or up to Lubeck to work in the marzipan factories, or the shipyards at Kiel; that's the way things are these days. All money. Nobody wants to work, just collect a wage packet once a week for doing as little as possible. Tourists? – At the moment? – Very few. There was an American couple over at the *gasthof* – but according to Frau Hermann – the Hermanns ran the place – they were only waiting for their daughter and son-in-law to come tomorrow to make up their party, then they were driving south to Bavaria where their son was stationed with the American Air Force. And there was a French family at the *pension* – the one behind the church. They were to be here for a week; the husband was an ornithologist and the wife a photographer. They were writing a book between them. South of here were marshlands, always a favourite place with people interested in birds. Perhaps by lunchtime the place would come to life for a little while. The *gasthof* wasn't exactly five-star but the food *was* good and the cellar cool, and tourists passing through, especially at weekends, used it for a waterhole, as it were. Maps? Yes. He did sell maps. As the *herr* could see, he sold *everything*. Only by diversifying his stocks could he survive. All he did not sell was alcohol – but then the *gasthof* did not sell camping-gas. You understand?

He walked across the stone setts of the square. Another car had arrived, an elderly Volkswagen Beetle, parked half on the pavement in front of the hotel, and a young man was hauling a couple of suitcases out of the back seat. An equally young woman stood by to help him. They looked like honeymooners.

In the hotel lobby a pleasant smell of cooking reminded him how hungry he was. There was no one at the desk, and the only sign of life was a cigarette burning in an ashtray below the counter. The décor was Gothically sombre, panelled walls, an antlered deer-head peering down above the till, a faded coat of arms of Schleswig-Holstein on the far wall. The young couple followed him in and put their suitcases on the floor behind him.

A curtain was briefly drawn aside behind the reception-desk and a man appeared with the air of being the proprietor. He was short and heavily built, in waistcoat and shirtsleeves and half-moon spectacles.

Coast, with a smile, stood aside and let the young couple go in front of him. Herr and Frau Beck. From Hanover. Here for three days. A double-room with bathroom. Booked over the telephone three weeks ago. Both of them too young and too starry-eyed to be anything other than they purported to be. The swag-bellied man watched Herr Beck sign the register, then handed over a room-key and slapped a desk-bell to summon someone to help them upstairs with their luggage.

He peered over the top of his spectacles at Coast.

'You require a room?'

'For one night only. Overlooking the *platz*, if you have one.'

'We have only a double.'

'I'll take it.'

The register was shoved forward. Above Beck's entry was one for a Mr. and Mrs. Savory of Greenboro, North Carolina, USA, and below that an entry for an Anton Gruber of Linz, Austria. Gruber had arrived last night, clearly unobserved by the keeper of the store across the square. There had been no other new arrivals at the hotel since Tuesday.

While Coast had been filling in the register, the taciturn Hermann had been copying the details of Tavistock's passport into a notebook that was kept under the counter. He returned the passport with a room-key on top of it.

'I'd like to pay in advance,' Coast said. 'I may have to leave early in the morning.'

'A charge is made for breakfast – if it is taken or not. Lunch and the evening meal are paid for at the time. – For the bed and breakfast it is one hundred and ten marks; with the tax. The room is on the left at the top of the stairs.'

Coast counted out notes while Hermann wrote a receipt.

He was half way up the stairs when the man called after him.

'Do you have luggage, Herr Tavistock?'

'In my car. I'll manage it myself.'

The man shrugged, stubbed out the burning cigarette, and returned to the mysteries behind the curtain.

He took lunch, sitting himself at a corner table, close to the door so that he could observe all the comings and goings without being too conspicuous. Like the honeymooning Becks, the Savorys looked no more or less what the storekeeper had said they were. He was a tall string-bean of a man with pebble-lensed spectacles, and she a homely-looking woman with a grey-blue rinse. Several other couples came in, who were obviously passing trade, but apart from himself no one sat alone who might have been Anton

Gruber from Linz. For no other reason than Gruber was here by himself, he had to be bracketted with the possible opposition.

For the first hour after lunch he reconnoitred the alleys and side streets of the village. There were plenty of cars in the square by now, and enough tourists moving about for him to escape notice as anything other than one of them.

Beyond the confines of the square Mildenheim simply petered out in every direction, although to the east it ended more abruptly against a screen of woodland with a narrow road of disintegrating concrete passing through it and its verges so overgrown that it was scarcely more than a footpath. Built before the war, perhaps, it had long since lost its purpose. At one point, through the trees, he glimpsed a heap of rusted metal that might once have been a Volkswagen.

He came to the border after only a few minutes. Suddenly and without warning there were no trees, only hacked-off stumps, and fifty yards into the clear space ahead of him stood the wire fence of the West German frontier, twelve feet high and seemingly impenetrable, with notices warning of mines beyond should anyone try to cut a way through to the other side. Another, similar fence stood dismally a hundred yards to the east, and he could clearly see a glint of glass as two green-uniformed guards in a watchtower kept an eye in the direction of Mildenheim. Between the two sets of wire the trees had been sawn down to ground level, so that all that showed of each was a few inches of stump like a decayed tooth. Nothing could pass over them without being spotted by the guards in the wooden tower. One thing was certain. Wherever Borisenko was to come across, it would not be here.

Fifteen

At five o'clock he went down to the reception desk to see if there had been any calls or visitors for him. The hotel lay in silence. At one end of the desk, a glossy grey cat briefly glanced at him before resuming the toilet it had been engaged upon before his interruption.

The register lay open. All he had to do was turn it. The Savorys had checked out. And beneath his own entry now was another. An H.A. Raikonnen, from Helsinki. He swiftly turned the register back the way it had been as someone came in from the street. And with an expectancy he could not disguise turned to see if the new arrival might be Dennikin.

But it was not. It was a small plump man, dabbing at a perspiring forehead with a handkerchief in one hand, while in the other, curiously out of keeping with his dark business-suit, he carried what appeared to be a petrol-driven chainsaw wrapped in black polythene sheeting.

'Not the day for carting one of those about,' Coast remarked as the little man came up beside him.

'Certainly isn't.' With a grunt, the little man hefted his machine on to the counter. 'But that's progress for you. Half the weight, twice the power. Would you believe it, even in this dump of a place I've taken orders for eight. And that's just today.' He popped his handkerchief into his breast pocket and tucked it out of sight with a couple of fingers. 'God, I could do with a beer. – Not in timber are you, by any chance? No land you want to clear?' With the deft touch of a conjurer he produced a business-card.

'Gruber. Of Gruber and Grosz. Nicely alliterative, eh. Of Linz. Importers and factors of timber felling machinery. This is Swedish. Runs all day on a half-litre of gasoline. Vibrates a bit – that's one of the penalties of cutting down on the weight of course. – Look, you may or may not believe this, but this machine … '

Well, he certainly wasn't Dennikin. He was Anton Gruber of Linz, loquacious seller of the latest thing in chainsaws. The one to watch for now was Raikonnen the Finn.

For the hour before dinner he sat in a wooden armchair by the window overlooking the street. Several cars drove into the square, but all passed on through. By eight-thirty it was dusk and there was still no sign of Dennikin. From where he sat, the sombre war-memorial was scarcely more than twenty-five yards away. It would be easy for a trained man with a telescopic sight to draw a bead on anything that moved down there. Not that Dennikin would be that crude. The death of Borisenko would happen somewhere else, on the road to Lubeck, somewhere out on the heathland north of here. Just so long as he himself was not implicated. The how and when was down to Dennikin.

He went downstairs soon after nine o'clock. The only other occupant of the dining-room was Gruber, who looked up hopefully as Coast came in, but returned to his newspaper when Coast ignored him and sat at the corner table he had used at lunchtime.

A meal that a week ago he might have enjoyed, tonight he could only toy with. He kept expecting at any moment to be called into the reception-lobby to keep the appointment with Dennikin. But at half-past nine he still had not come. Nor did Raikonnen, if that was his real name, put in an appearance in the dining-room.

Not until ten did Coast start to feel uneasy. If Dennikin had left Paris at midday Thursday he should have been here by now. He ordered another beer. Gruber, with his newspaper under his arm, went out into the lobby, and after stopping briefly at the desk carried on upstairs. The waitress took away the coffee-cup and beer-glass from where he had been sitting.

The young couple he had guessed to be honeymooning came down shortly afterwards and looked faintly surprised at the lateness of the hour. The waitress, at first, was not disposed to serve them anything but sandwiches, but then Hermann came to see what the fuss was about and the two of them were soon sitting down to a three-course meal and smiling vapidly at each other between mouthfuls. They looked settled in for the night.

He ordered another coffee. At half-past ten, another. It was soon after that that the waitress went upstairs and came down again shortly afterwards with a tray with a half-eaten meal and an empty wine-glass on it. Mr. Raikonnen had taken dinner in his room. Not that there was anything sinister in that, unless Mr. Raikonnen was either a watcher or was avoiding being watched. But what he certainly was – an unknown quantity – encouraged a little more unease, a sensation that fed upon itself so that he had to consciously control his tendency to fidget.

For half an hour then, he sat out in the lobby, ostensibly reading a newspaper, but listening, poised for the sound of a car pulling up outside, a footfall on the steps up from the street. Several times the light of headlamps flickered like quicksilver across the square, but no cars stopped, no one came up the steps.

He folded the newspaper and went across to the desk. The hotel register still lay open on the counter. The honeymooners were in Room 6, next to his own, Raikonnen in Room 3; exactly opposite him.

'Something I can do for you, Herr Tavistock?'

Caught unawares, there was nothing he could do but keep his hand on the register and put on an anxious scowl as Hermann let the curtain fall behind him.

'Forgive me,' he said. 'I didn't want to bother you. But I'm waiting for a business colleague. A Herr Soderstrom – a Swede. I was checking to see if he might have booked in yet.'

'No, Herr Tavistock. No one of that name. Sorry.'

'When do you close?'

'We don't. – A night-porter comes in at midnight. If your

Herr Soderstrom turns up, if you wish, he will wake you.'

'Thank you.'

Coast returned to his newspaper. Hermann picked up a ledger he had come for and went back behind the red curtain.

The quarter after eleven came and went. A heavy lorry trundled into the square, and with a racket of clumsy gear-changing took the road out again. After a while the sound of it died. There were only forty-five minutes left of the day. Not even that. Forty-two.

He put down the newspaper and picked up another.

The Becks came dewy-eyed from the dining-room and went slowly upstairs.

At some indeterminate time – for all his looking at his watch, if he had been asked the time a second afterwards he would have had to look at his watch again – it occurred to him that he was alone here, that Dennikin would not be coming. A hold up at the frontier, an accident. Shapeless thoughts at first, one hard upon the other. Borisenko would step into Peterson's car out there in the square tomorrow morning, and he would be utterly powerless to stop them. By lunch-time Borisenko would be sitting in the room in Lubeck, surrounded by tape-recorders and CIA interrogators, bleating for all he was worth.

It was a moment he had dreaded for years. The chance he had always chosen to gamble against. Someone coming over with a list of names. Not that arrests could ever be made on the mere word of a defector. But seeds were sown, watchers put to work, history remorselessly dug up, the jigsaw patiently assembled.

'Still up, then?'

It was Gruber, if he really was Gruber, just in from the street, needlessly wiping his feet on the coconut mat by the door.

'Still waiting for your Swedish chap?'

Coast smiled up benignly at him. 'You listen at too many keyholes, Herr Gruber.'

But Gruber's hide was thicker than that. 'I was on my way downstairs when you were asking our friend the innkeeper.

Couldn't help overhearing.' He had come closer, and was putting on a pair of reading-glasses he had taken from inside his jacket. 'Don't suppose there's a *Hamburger Zeitung* in that pile, is there?' He leaned over the heap of papers and magazines on the coffee-table and rummaged through them until he found what he wanted. Tucking it under his arm as he straightened up, he said: 'All the 'planes are running a couple of hours late out of Stockholm; I heard it earlier on the local radio. They had an accident there round about five o'clock this afternoon. For what it's worth.'

'He isn't coming from Stockholm,' Coast said. 'But thank you.'

Gruber at last took the hint.

'See you at breakfast,' he said. 'Goodnight.'

Coast watched him go, then lifted aside his cuff. It was tomorrow.

He lay upon the bed in the dark, listening to the old timbers of the hotel creak as they gave up the heat of the day to the cool of the small hours. His cigarette traced a glowing arc as it passed to and from his mouth. A few minutes ago, on Gruber's side, a window had been slammed shut. On the honeymooners' side all was quiet.

Somewhere along the line the operation had been torpedoed. Perhaps at the East German end. Perhaps Borisenko hadn't made it across the border after all. Perhaps Dennikin had instructions to make hourly routine calls back to Paris for up-dates on the latest state of affairs, and had been recalled.

At one o'clock, alert and tense, he was again at the window looking down into the square. This time tomorrow he would be back in London, nothing accomplished. So much for Centre's organisation, its much vaunted omnipotence.

He put another cigarette between his lips, lit it, and tilted his watch-face towards his lighter. The hours were racing, the minutes crawling. It was five past one.

Down in the square what looked like a page of newspaper cartwheeled desultorily for a few yards and came to a stop against the step of the war-memorial. A light still shone from Gruber's window next door. Reading his *Hamburg Zeitung?* Or listening?

The last of the sand was running out of the glass. With each passing minute the chances of Dennikin turning up became more remote. If he didn't come soon ...

A door-latch clicked softly somewhere out in the passage. Not Gruber's, not the Becks', further away than that. Raikonnen. It would be Raikonnen, the last of the unknown quantities. The room was only lit by what little light spilled in from the square and he cracked his knee on the side of the dressing-table as he turned for the door. It lost him the vital couple of seconds he needed; so that all he saw was the bathroom door closing, and a pencil of light come on beneath it.

With his door open to a slit, he heard water running, the toilet flushing, then silence. There was no light under the door of the room opposite.

He waited several minutes. Water gurgled out of a sink, several paper towels were ripped out of the machine behind the door. The toilet was flushed again. Then another silence while the rush of water subsided to a whisper. He could feel his heart pounding and was suddenly conscious that he was holding his breath.

The light went out beneath the bathroom door. The door-lever soundlessly rotated. The door opened. He hastily closed his own back to a slit.

The man was in trousers and singlet and socks. Short, thin to the point of emaciation. Carrying a stick. Had a limp. Good leg, stick, good leg, stick. He moved in little hops, furtive, quick. In his other hand, something glittered. A razor – it looked like – the old-fashioned kind, a cut-throat.

Coast silently closed the door until he was sure the man had reached his own door and had his back to him; then opened it again against the toe of his shoe. The man was feeling awkwardly into his pocket for his room key, while his other hand clutched both stick and razor. And for a second, after he had steered the key into the lock, he glanced towards the stairs to the lobby, and for that second was in profile. A thin gaunt face, round-shouldered.

Nikky Borisenko.

He thrust another cigarette impatiently into his mouth and lit it with a shaking hand. The castellans at Centre had really left the gate open this time. Borisenko was here and Dennikin was not.

They had betrayed him.

The backs of his legs found the edge of the bed. He sank to it.

He was going to have to kill Borisenko himself.

He watched the red stain lighten in the sky to the east. It was a quarter to five.

He reached out to switch off the lamp on the cabinet beside the bed. He had a few times during the night fallen asleep but only ever lightly and never for long. An hour ago he had gone across to the bathroom. His bladder would have to last out now until he got to Hamburg. The essence of everything was silence.

He shaved with the body of his electric-razor muffled by a sock, and using the mirror on the back of the open wardrobe door. That done, he put the razor in its box and checked his overnight bag to make sure he had packed absolutely everything. Then for the second time quartered the room with a sock over his hand in the gathering light and wiped over everything he could possibly have touched. The door-lever, light-switch, the switch and stem on the lamp beside the bed, the wall-socket where he had plugged in his shaver. The ashtray he had already emptied in the bathroom. He hadn't smoked since. He checked his pockets. Passport, wallet, air-line tickets, keys.

It was a couple of minutes after five o'clock. He put on Tavistock's spectacles.

A moment by the door to summon up the last reserve of the nerve it was going to take to knock at Borisenko's door and face him. He had formulated no plan other than to get into Borisenko's room. After that it was all going to be on a catch as catch can basis. And abruptly he was cold, dispassionate, knew he could do it.

With his hand in his pocket, he worked the door-lever through the lining of his jacket.

Crossed the now vast expanse of passage.

Found a creaking floorboard. For a moment stood perfectly still.

From somewhere higher up in the hotel came the muffled sound of an alarm-clock ringing. It would not be long before the staff was up and about.

He raised a knuckle to the panel of Borisenko's door. Cast one look back over his shoulders towards Gruber's room – he still had doubts about Gruber – and one more towards the stairs down to the lobby on the look-out for the night-porter.

Two brief raps with the knuckle of a forefinger, banking on Borisenko being as wide awake as he was.

The alarm-clock had stopped ringing.

'*Wer da?*'

The voice had come suddenly, muted, through the door. It startled him. There was still time to back down, steal back to his own room, fly back to London.

He rapped again, only once, as if he hadn't heard. Rouse Borisenko's curiosity; lure him to open the door.

'*Wer da?*'

Coast put his mouth close to the corner of door and frame.

'Minaret.' A long-shot. One of the few things he had rehearsed. For hours he had lain awake making plans, but each was so shot through with flaws that in the end he had abandoned all of them. Just to get into that room with Borisenko was the first step. The second would look after itself.

An eternity passed. A key went into the door-lock. The door opened an inch, no more than Borisenko needed to take stock with one eye. And he would have his foot behind the door to stop it being barged open. It was a temptation to rush him. But instead Coast waited tensely until the single eye in the pale gaunt cheek came suspiciously to rest. Unmistakeably Borisenko.

'Who are you?'

Coast was ready for that. From his jacket he took out Tavistock's passport and held it open under Borisenko's nose.

'Tavistock,' he said. 'British. Assistant-Consul. Hamburg.'

That cut no ice.

'You must have the wrong person. My name is Raikonnen.'

Coast shoved his foot against the bottom of the door as it started to close.

'Peterson can't make it. I've come to take you to Lubeck.'

He felt some of the pressure go off the door.

' – And the other name I was told to give you is Dennikin.'

'I know of no Dennikin.'

'KGB. Their Paris station. We know he reached Ratzeburg late last night. We think he's coming this way.'

From within the room was only silence. A toilet flushed upstairs.

'What has happened to Peterson?'

More pressure had gone off the door.

'I don't know. All I know is that he can't be contacted and I've been given half an hour to get you out of here.'

'You were here last night, Mr. Tavistock. I saw your name in the register.'

'I'm only here as a fall-back. I only knew what I was here for an hour ago. Now for Christ's sake let me in. If Dennikin arrives before I can get you out you're very likely dead. – Please!'

The door opened wider. Borisenko backed away, leaning on his stick, hop, step, hop, step. His curtains were open. No luggage, just a jacket and a shirt on a chair, a pair of shoes on the floor, the razor on the dressing-table. He had travelled light. And he stood a yard out of reach, frail of body but sharp of eye.

'I wasn't told you'd be carrying a stick.'
'I have sprained my ankle. It is nothing serious.'

For perhaps half a minute then Borisenko continued to weigh him. And still he did not ask the one pertinent question. Then slowly, braced on his stick, he backed towards the chair where his jacket and shirt were. The moment he dropped his gaze, Coast was going to jump him, but Borisenko's eyes never shifted once. He felt for his shirt, and when he found it transferred his stick to his other hand and wriggled one arm into it.

There would be the one chance, and only the one. Soon.

'May I help you?'

'No, thank you.'

Borisenko changed hands on the stick and the other arm went into the shirt. He shrugged it across his shoulders and fastened the buttons expertly with his left hand. That day by the river he had flung pebbles with his left hand. – And still he did not ask the one question.

He tucked his shirt into his trousers, leisurely, unhurried, watchful. And now dangerous. Dangerous because he had known better than to ask the question. What Borisenko had done was to buy time for himself because he already knew the answer, but he had left it marginally too long and Coast was already bearing down on him as Borisenko reached for his jacket and whatever it was in the pocket of it thudded against the frame of the chair; and he was still diving a hand into the pocket that was heavy as Coast slammed him back against the wall and drove the breath out of him.

Coast felt the tangle of the jacket about his feet as it fell between them. He had twisted the stick out of Borisenko's hand – but there was no space to wield it – screwing up a handful of Borisenko's shirt he swung him away from the wall. Momentum carried them both towards the bed. Something struck him high up on the cheekbone, then again lower down, the last a puny, glancing blow. They struggled in silence, inexpertly, like schoolboys. The heel of Borisenko's hand thrust up under Coast's chin, but there was no strength in it. Coast's weight told. Straddling Borisenko he pinioned him across the bed, with a quick jerk had the walking stick across Borisenko's throat and thrust his whole weight forward and down on it while Borisenko's hands scrabbled for his face; and when that was ineffectual tried to get his hands around the stick and lift it off. But he didn't have the strength. Breath gobbled in his throat as he fought for air.

Coast ignored the blinding pain that lanced into his groin. Nothing mattered any more. He had to go on. It was such a scrawny little throat. He bore down, all his weight.

It was done. Borisenko's eyes stared out at nothing and there was a deep dark depression across his throat with the pattern of the walking-stick in it.

Coast's own breath still sawed in and out. There wasn't a part of him that wasn't shaking. The gun lay on the pillow, a small black automatic.

It was a long time before he was able to do anything. Then, at last, like a breathless trembling lover he climbed off Borisenko. Little enough in life, in death he had shrunk to nothing.

Borisenko's jacket was still on the floor between the windows. Coast ransacked the pockets, turning the contents out on to the dressing-table. A cheap plastic wallet, banknotes, mostly German, a few that were Finnish. A passport – Finnish – a concertina of credit-cards almost identical to his own – some coins, all German – a bunch of keys. Nothing else. And there *had* to be something else. With a stab of one of the keys he slashed through the jacket's lining and rent it, then again, then tore it apart. Nothing. There were no signs of luggage, not even a lightweight bag. There was nothing in the wardrobe or dressing-table. He hauled all the drawers out, looked at their backs and bottoms, peered into the recesses on his hands and knees. It was twenty-past five.

There was a cabinet beside the bed like the one in his own room. He searched that, had the lining-paper out of the drawer, had the entire thing away from the wall and tipped it over.

The edges of the carpet had been tacked down every few inches. Hadn't been touched.

He went back to Borisenko's inert body sprawled across the bed. There was a spreading damp stain of urine fast blackening the front of the dark trousers. The pockets were warm and damp and revolting. Only a handkerchief in one. The other was empty. He checked each of the shoes. Well-worn solid heels, nothing stuffed up the toes or in the linings.

Twenty-five past five and someone was moving about upstairs. No more time, nowhere else to look. He spent a few minutes more restoring the room to some semblance of order and getting Borisenko's body under the bedclothes; when he put his hands under its armpits the body gave up the last of its wind like a belch of indigestion. He turned it so that it faced away from the door, and when he dragged up the covers over it, it gave a reasonable appearance of being only asleep. Then with the sock over his hand again like a mitten he wiped over everything he could remember touching. The pistol went down into the bed with Borisenko, the coins into his own pocket, the wallet too, and the passport.

One last glance about. The room looked orderly. The stick. It was hooked over the end of the bed. It was the one thing he hadn't checked. But it was only a stick, a solid hawthorn with a rubber ferrule that he feverishly wrestled off and wrestled back on again. Nothing unscrewed.

It was still quiet in the passage. He transferred the key from the inside of the door to the outside. The DO NOT DISTURB sign was an afterthought. He hung it over the door-lever on the outside, softly turned the key and took it out and dropped it into his pocket. He would lose that somewhere along the road.

In his room, he transferred Borisenko's passport and wallet to his overnight bag, stuffing both in under the plywood stiffener at the bottom. It was all hurriedly done, a minute at most. Then out for the last time to the passage, the sock over his hand, not locking the door this time because

A Position of Trust

two locked rooms on the same landing would be too much of a coincidence.

Down the stairs to the lobby, not too quickly. No one about. A clatter of crockery from the kitchen – probably the night-porter – the door to the square wide open and wedged back with a corner of the coconut mat to let the air in.

And he was out, crossing the square in the long dawn shadows, aware that he was precipitously close to the edge of panic and that only will-power was stopping him going over.

A couple of hours and he would be in Hamburg. A needle in a haystack. Safe.

In the rear-view mirror he watched the green and white Ford pull in behind him on the layby, and the driver climb out putting on his white-topped summer cap.

It had been a mistake to stop here. He was still twenty minutes out of Hamburg. His nerve had gone and the last straw had been the articulated lorry that bored past him on the inside lane with its horn blowing and all but forced him up on to the central reservation and the crash-barrier. That had been a kilometre back. He had pulled in here to gather his wits and try to calm down a little. His hands had been trembling so much that he had had difficulty lighting a cigarette. Only in the last minute or so had he begun to feel capable of grasping the wheel again.

The white shirt and uniform trousers loomed larger in the door mirror until all he could see was a black belt and a revolver-holster. He tensed as a youthful face peered in at the open window. It smelled of aftershave; and even as it cheerfully smiled and a tanned hand rose to touch the black visor of its cap it swept a single comprehensive glance over the inside of the car.

'Trouble, *mein herr*? Or are you taking a break?'

Coast felt the skin shrink over the backs of his hands.

'Just a break,' he said. He smiled back. 'I've been driving all night.'

'Ah, so.' The smile that broke then was of brotherly understanding. 'Then that is why all your lights are on. I thought you were waiting for a breakdown truck.'

'No. Nothing like that.' Where the hell was the light-switch – that one. He must have switched it on inadvertently, earlier, in his hurry to get out of the square. A deep-blue indicator-light went out on the dashboard. In the sunlight he hadn't noticed it on. 'Thank you for telling me.'

'All part of the service, *mein herr*. Good-day to you. Drive carefully.'

The cap visor was touched again and the policeman returned to his patrol car, pistol bouncing against one hip, a radio on the other.

Coast reached for the ignition-key. That was one confrontation he could well have done without.

Sixteen

With a sickening upward lurch the aircraft lifted off. It was dead on time.

He had left the Escort on the first floor of a multi-storey car park near Dammtor railway station, and Borisenko's keys were now stuffed down behind the seat of the taxi that had brought him to the airport. It might be days before they were found and even then it was doubtful if anyone would make the connection. And back in Mildenheim the German police would be putting two and two together by now and it would not be long before they were blocking off the harbours and airports and frontier posts in their search for a missing Englishman. For another hour he was going to have to sweat it out. Once down at Heathrow and Tavistock would disappear from the face of the earth.

The aircraft levelled off and the smoking-light came on. He had killed. The ultimate response to fear. A response triggered by the sudden realisation that the slab of metal in Borisenko's jacket was a gun. If it hadn't been for that he might never have carried it through. And Borisenko had never asked the pertinent question because it was less of a risk to shoot first. And guess the answer afterwards.

For a while he made a show of reading a magazine, but the spectacles blurred the fine print and his fingers stuck to the glossy pages. When a stewardess came along the aisle with her tray of mid-flight drinks he resisted the temptation. There was still too much left to do. The first was to make for Charing Cross station and contact Michael, spell out the situation, demand help. They owed him that. Then he had to call in at Victoria and collect his briefcase. And over the next few days the suit he was wearing would have to be lost somewhere, and the overnight bag as well – too many people had seen both, including the patrolman on the autobahn.

The Thames estuary glittered under a heat haze beneath the starboard wing. Another quarter of an hour and the aircraft would be touching down. His only fear now was that the German authorities had alerted London and that down there someone was waiting for Mr. Tavistock to come through Immigration.

He went through Customs on the green. No one stopped him. Out at the other end he made straight for the nearest toilets; and when after half-an-hour he came out again Tavistock was as dead as Borisenko. When he checked his appearance in a mirror over one of the handbasins he saw the small yellow stain of a ripening bruise where Borisenko had struck him with either the barrel or the butt of the pistol he had been carrying. At the time he had scarcely felt it.

It was almost two o'clock of the afternoon when the taxi turned into the forecourt of Charing Cross station, and at Battersea Michael was waiting for him. Less than five minutes went by before he was ringing back.

'What has happened?'

'It was a balls-up. I want to meet. I can be in Hampstead by three o'clock.'

'I shall be there. – But I have to know about Borisenko.'

'He's dead. I killed him. – I tell you, it was a balls-up.'

There was a stunned silence from the other end.

'You? So where was Dennikin?'

'God knows. I don't. – I'll see you in Hampstead.'

Out in the forecourt the only taxi on the rank was the one he had arrived in, and because it was important to break his trail he walked as far as Whitehall and hailed another.

Michael was early. Pale faced and discomposed he led Coast into the long lounge that looked out over the Heath.

'You look tired,' he said.

'I am.' Coast dropped his briefcase and the overnight bag on the floor beside one of the armchairs, then sat down on the arm of it. Michael took a leather cigarette-case out of his jacket and proffered it. They were English cigarettes today, not his usual black ones with the cardboard tips. Coast plucked one out. He wondered if his hands would ever stop shaking. Michael struck his lighter and held it down to the tip of the cigarette. 'You must try to relax,' he said. 'Would you like a drink?'

'Scotch. A large one.'

Michael made himself free with a cluster of decanters on a galleried silver tray on a corner-table by the window. He brought back a substantial whisky, and a smaller vodka for himself, both in cut-crystal tumblers. He held out the whisky. Coast took it. The first mouthful bit, and scalded his throat. Michael stood watching until the tumbler was half empty before taking down nearly all of his vodka at a single swallow.

'We have already been in touch with Moscow on the radio,' he said. 'They have instructed us to de-brief you. Every detail. Everything you are able to remember. I am sorry, but it is necessary. Do you feel up to it?'

'There is no hurry,' Michael went on. 'If you wish, there is nothing to stop you sleeping for an hour first. The bed here is comfortable.'

'No, thank you. I'd rather get it done with.'

Michael weighed him from under his eyebrows. He took another sip of his vodka, then turned away and went to stand with his back to the screened-off fireplace.

'We were warned by our doctors in Moscow that you would be in shock – and that something would have to be done about that – for your own safety, I hasten to add. – A few hours with a pretty girl. To relax. To wind you down, as you say ... '

'Joke.'

'My friend it is either that or drugs. – In an hour – two – you could break down altogether. – You would not want that and neither do we. – So it is not a joke. – You will need to talk to someone. – The locks safely on the doors. And afterwards she will see you safely home and forget all about you.'

The whisky glass clattered against his teeth again. He was cold. All over cold.

'You're sure?'

'I am sure. She is one of us.'

He emptied the glass and held it out.

'Get her,' he said. ' – And fill this fucking thing again, will you?'

'And he did not ask how you recognised him?'

'No. – He didn't need to. – He was going to fucking kill me anyway. – Whatever I was, I was a bloody risk he couldn't afford to take. – I never thought about that ... '

'My friend, relax.' Michael rose and took Coast's glass again and half filled it. 'It is over. Done with. – Start from there. Slowly. Everything you are able to remember.'

He remembered everything down to the last detail, details that he had not taken in even at the time, the sudden ammoniacal stench of urine that Borisenko had given off, the texture of the walking-stick, the warm male smell of the bedclothes, the pattern on the butt of the autobahn patrolman's pistol.

'How long did he talk to you?'

'I don't remember. – A few minutes.'

'Had you done anything to make him suspicious?'

'No. I'd left the bloody head-lights on, that's all.'

'Then you have nothing to worry about.'

'I bloody well hope so.'

'My friend, believe me, everything will be all right. We shall look after you.'

'So you keep telling me.' He held out the glass to be refilled. It was his fourth and Michael was pouring doubles and it was doing nothing for him.

*

Then back over it all again. It was four o'clock.

'And this is all he had?' Michael made a gesture to take in Borisenko's few effects on the settee beside him. The passport, the wallet, the plastic concertina of credit cards. 'You are sure?'

'I'm sure.'

'And what about the people at the hotel? Were any of them CIA, do you think?'

'Christ knows.'

Then back over it all yet again, the same questions, the same responses.

'Did you check it; this stick?'

'It was new, I told you. Solid.'

'Did you think to check the bandage around his ankle?'

'No, I didn't. There wasn't time.'

'You should have.'

'Oh, for Christ's sake!'

'Relax.' Michael held up a staying hand. 'My friend relax. I can imagine what this has done to you.' He glanced at his watch. 'In ten minutes the girl will come and I shall go. We are almost finished. All I want from you now is to know what you want from us.'

'A new passport.'

'You shall have it. The end of the week.'

'Sooner.'

'My friend, I am sorry. They are made to order at Centre. It will take a week.'

'A bolt-hole – somewhere to hide if the Special Branch come sniffing.'

'Easy. Ring Battersea. I will have you picked up from wherever you choose within an hour.'

'That bag, and everything in it goes; except the shaver.'

'Done. It will all go in the Embassy incinerator. I shall take it with me.'

'An out. Planned. No balls-ups.'

'Also done.'

'And Dennikin.'

Michael narrowed his eyes.

'If Dennikin cannot explain, *you* will not have Dennikin. *We* shall.' Then Michael's face slackened into a smile and he made a showier business of looking at his watch. 'I suggest you have a shower now, my friend. A shave also. Put yourself in the mood. There is no longer any hurry to do anything. Simply relax. – And we shall look after you.'

He screwed his eyes shut and held his face up to the sprinkler and let the cascade of steaming water lash over him. A ritual, a symbolic cleansing.

The door-bell buzzed four times in quick succession as at last he turned off the water and felt about for the towel. His body on the outside tingled with heat, but on the inside still shivered with an icy cold. Michael let the woman in, and for the time it took him to towel himself dry the two of them were talking softly and quickly in Russian in the lobby. Then Michael was going, the door closing behind him, the snick of the door-latch. The woman's light tread went into the bedroom, surely, because, like Michael, she was on familiar ground here; and because she was the unseen she was also the unknown and he felt again the first small pricklings of fear.

He shaved meticulously, and with great concentration. The face he saw in the mirror, apart from the small bruise high up on one cheek, was no different from the one he had shaved yesterday, or the day before that, or last week. And half of him knew that this dullness he felt now would pass. It was a nervous reaction. An anaesthetic. Tomorrow was going to be bad, and the day after that worse. That fear came in many guises and more often in the dead hours of the night, and that the worst fear was the fear of being alone with the fear.

The woman was in the lounge now, drawing closed the curtains, switching on a few strategically placed lights, turning day into night and setting the scene. And his prick twitched despite himself. They had always been his weakness, women.

Then, as meticulously as he had shaved with it, he blew the razor out over the handbasin and washed away the grey-brown powdery dust in a swill of cold water. Tomorrow, he was going to ring Michael from Charing Cross station, ask – demand if he had to – beg if he had to – for an out. Somewhere in the East. The grace and favour apartment in one of Moscow's drab concrete blocks, the pension they had always promised him, the sinecure of a job of some sort in Dzerzhinski Square. He had given twenty years of his life, and the lives of two other men on top of that. And they owed him. And what surfaced then, surpassing even the fear and the need for sex, was anger. They had let him down, forced him into a corner, and for that he would never forgive them.

He girded himself in the towelling bath-robe that Michael had sorted out from somewhere and padded barefoot into the lounge. Only the wall lights and one standard lamp were on. It might have been night.

The woman was pouring a drink from one of the decanters on the galleried silver tray. The sex-machine they had sent along to keep him quiet.

'*S'drasvuti*,' she said, smiling along her shoulder at him with a bright whore's smile as if she had known him for ever. ' – I am Irena. – And you are Anton, ni'? – And you drink Scotch whisky, I think.'

'A double. Then some.'

She put down one decanter and picked up another. 'Michael has told you that you may be free to talk to me, ni'? – I know what you had to do for all of us this morning. We are very grateful, and I will do my best to help you forget, ni'? Make a pleasant evening for you.'

She stoppered the decanter and carefully set it back on the silver tray, then, with a crystal tumbler depending from the thumb and forefinger of each hand, stalked towards him like a beautifully articulated piece of machinery. What little she wore, the statutory tube of black lingerie, the flesh stockings, the strappy Bond Street shoes and a wristwatch, she carried with sufficient unconcern to have sailed her across the foyer of the Savoy and half-way up the stairs before anyone might have noticed that she had forgotten to put on a dress.

'And you fuck, ni'?'

She sipped at her drink and flashed another toothpaste-commercial smile at him.

'Oh, yes,' she agreed equably. 'I fuck all right. – Talk, fuck, body-massage – some blue-video – it is whatever you want. – I do not mind.' She looked him up and down like the public hangman assessing his frame and weight to get the length of rope and the drop exactly right. ' – Make many nice comes for you. – Three – four times, perhaps.'

He took down a slug of whisky and measured her the way she had measured him, the shapely muscular legs, the broad hips, the pneumatic bust, the swimmer's shoulders, the cascade of blonde hair that looked like a wig.

'You'd bloody better,' he said. 'You owe me. You and your lot owe me.'

And it was killing Borisenko all over again. He buried his face between her scented legs and made her squirm and wriggle and swear and moan and screw her fingers into the sheets the way the best whores do and she faked a couple of orgasms then had a real one with her legs clamped hard on his face. Now you give me prick, ni'? You give it to me, ni'. And it was like a rage. Oh, you fuck good, you hurt me, oh, Jesus, and she swore, swore some more and she wriggled some more and raked her sharp heels down his legs. I fucking come again – oh – and she closed her teeth on his shoulder and dug her nails into his back and it was all charades and tricks of the light and her sex closed about him like a fistful of honey and it was all as potent as rot-gut moonshine.

And for a long time afterwards he couldn't move, couldn't breathe, thought he was going to die – and didn't care.

And one of her hands swept through his hair like a comb and just for a moment it felt like love.

'We eat now, ni'? – Have a little rest, ni'? – Get sexy again. I do nice massage for you, make you very excite, make mouth for you. Make you come so you never stop. I do that for you, ni'?'

And his prick jerked. 'Yes,' he said. 'You do that. You do that good, ni'?'

And now it was late, although how late he didn't know. Time was displaced. She was on his lap, the two of them jammed together in the one armchair, and in a neck to toe white lace body stocking she was more naked than naked and every time she stirred deeper into his lap a little more of him erected inside her in the flickering coloured half-dark. And when the beautiful blonde boy with the stallion's prick at last entered the dark Circassian girl, Irena, or whatever her name was, stirred him like porridge, and nestled in closer with a lace arm around his neck and whispered, 'Some horny prick that boy got, ni'. Like a fuckin' horse.'

And the dark Circassian girl sighed and yawned her legs wider and rammed her hips up to meet him. *Volischya*, she hissed. *Volischya*. – That means more – she wants some more, ni'? – And the beautiful blonde boy reared up on rigid muscular arms and withdrew an inch, then ruthlessly gave her all of it. And the girl gritted her teeth and reached up for his shoulders and moaned with delight before her hands fell helplessly down to the pillows and fluttered open like lilies. And the boy was slow and relentless and immensely powerful.

'They are good together ni'? – Look – see – make you come just to look ni'? He touch her only where it matters, ni'?'

And she was all lace and his prick burned inside her and one of her nipples had swollen through the lace and she was trembling with excitement, a sinuous lace clad snake. 'Lace better than skin ni'? Sexier, ni'? – Oh, yes. You come. All hot in there for you, ni'? You come all you want. – All you want. Then we hold close, ni'? Make talk. Sleep.'

Streatham at one o'clock in the morning was alien and unfamiliar through the windscreen of the Fiesta.

She reached over to the back seat for his briefcase and stood it on his lap.

'If you like, I will spend the rest of the night with you. – To keep you company.'

'No, thanks.'

'You will not do anything silly, ni'? – Like going to the nearest police-station and confessing?'

He didn't answer. Most of her ambiguous fractured accent was gone.

One of his hands was curled over the briefcase. Her warm one rose to cover it, pressed a folded scrap of paper between his fingers.

'You telephone me, ni'? – For sex – for talk – whatever you want. – Michael has told me to do that. – Also that he will press hard for your new passport. – Also to tell you that you have many friends. – I also am your friend. – What we do tonight, no one ever know. Is private. – Even Michael will not know.'

'I don't give a fuck,' he said, and swung his legs out of the car. 'You just make sure Michael gets me that passport. Pretty damn quick, ni'? Because if I go down, you all bloody well go down. You tell Michael that, ni'.'

The lift was out of order and he had to use the stairs; and the effort winded him so that he had to stop on each landing to get his breath. The need for violence to expunge violence had gone the moment he had slammed the door of the Fiesta. What was coming to him now was fear, the cold fingers scrabbling in his belly at the anticipation of tomorrow and the day after that.

Michael was going to have to get him out.

From light to darkness. When he pushed through the swing-doors on his landing there was blackness beyond them, and when he felt on the wall for the light-switch, and gave it a couple of flicks, that wasn't working either and he had to feel his way along the doors in the all-enveloping dark.

He took out his keys and fingered the serrations. The first one he tried was the wrong one. Then the hairs at the back of his neck began to tingle because he wasn't alone here in the dark. And he felt, rather than saw, the wide burly figure come from the recess in the wall where the extinguishers and buckets and fire-hoses were stored.

Then a small torch glowed, the sort of thing motorists have on a key-ring, to help him to see the keyhole.

'I think the bulb's gone, Mr. Coast,' the figure said as it drew closer. 'I hope I didn't startle you, sir. – Fairhazel – Special Branch. – You might remember me.'

Seventeen

He turned the key and reached around the door-frame for the light switch. They knew nothing. Couldn't. Not this soon.

Fairhazel followed him into the lounge. He was carrying a small aluminium case.

Coast smiled glassily through his fear.

'So what can I do for the thin blue line?'

The feeble joke fell dead.

'That, sir. Please, sir.'

That was the briefcase.

'Really? – And on whose authority? – I presume you do have some authority?'

'Enough, sir. – Mr. Mingay's at home right now. – If you like, you can give him a ring. I've got the number. Please, sir – if you don't mind.'

He handed over the briefcase. Remembered the piece of paper the girl had given him. He no longer had it, wondered if he had dropped it in the street, in the corridor, if it mattered.

' – And your passport, sir.'

So they did know something after all. Jesus.

'Passport? – No, of course you can't see my passport. Who the hell do you think you are, for Christ's sake?'

'The important thing is, sir, – are you carrying it? – Got it on you, have you?'

A loophole. Something in Fairhazel's voice. – *The important thing is, sir, are you carrying it?* He hoped – but he didn't *know*.

'Of course I'm not carrying it. Why should I be?'
'Not in your jacket, sir?'
'No; this is ridiculous. – Here, man, feel. – Frisk me if you like. – Get it over with.'

Fairhazel's hand touched his chest, each jacket pocket, the hip-pocket of his trousers.

'How about in here, sir? – The briefcase. Do you mind if I look?'

'Whatever the hell you like. – Then we both sit down together and you tell me what all this is about. Right? – Can I get you something. – No, of course, you can't, can you. – Do you mind if I do?'

'No, sir, you carry on.' Fairhazel was already unbuckling the briefcase.

A brittle chuckle to mask the clink of the bottle against the glass. 'What kind of a wild-goose chase are you on exactly, Mr. Fairhazel? – Do you know?'

He was feeling better now, more in charge. If he took it cautiously there might be a way out of all this.

When he turned around with the glass in his hand, Fairhazel was dominating the middle of the room, his eyes everywhere, taking it all in, costing, tagging, weighing everything, missing nothing. The open briefcase was on the table.

'Cheers.'

The cold face stayed cold.

'So where is it, sir? – Your passport?'

'In the bedroom.'

'If you wouldn't mind, then, sir. – I would like to see it.'

A few moments in the bedroom. Mercifully Fairhazel didn't follow him in there. Fishing. That's all they were doing. They weren't that efficient to be doing anything else.

Fairhazel had filled one of the armchairs, an elbow on the arm of it, a thumb pushed up under his chin.

'Here. – Look all you like.' He dropped the passport by Fairhazel's elbow.

'Thank you, sir.'

Fairhazel thumbed interestedly through the dog-eared pages. It took him some time.

Coast finished his drink and went to pour another, but measuring it carefully. The last one had been far too big for a man with nothing on his mind. Stupid, that.

'Do you mind if I keep this, sir?'

'Have you a warrant for it?'

'No, sir.'

'But you could get one? – Even at one o'clock in the morning?'

'If I had to.'

'And I've nothing to hide – so, yes. – You can keep it.'

'Thank you, Mr. Coast. – Saves a great deal of time for both of us. – I'm obliged to you.'

Fairhazel closed the passport and slipped it into his jacket. Made himself comfortable again, the ankle of one leg over the knee of the other.

'Can I ask where you've been?'

'When – exactly?'

'Since Friday.'

'Friday?'

'The newspaper in your briefcase was Friday's.'

For a moment he had thought they might have followed him to the airport on Friday evening.

'Yesterday, I was here all day.'

'I'm more interested in today.'

A chummy smile. We're all old boys together, know what it's all about, don't we?

' – Frankly, I'd rather not. Or is the Special Branch doing a bit of moonlighting these days for cuckolded husbands?'

That fell flat too.

'So what's the lady's name?'

The 'sirs' had been despatched. He noticed that particularly.

'Oh, come on, Superintendent, or Chief Superintendent, or whatever you bloody well are. – That one you don't get answered.'

Fairhazel smiled fractionally.

'We would only want a word with her. Discreet. A few minutes. A bit of slap and tickle on the side isn't on the statute-book yet. And we can get all the titillation we need from the Sunday newspapers.'

'No. – I'm sorry.'

'Perhaps the name of an hotel? The names you registered in? That would be enough.'

'No hotels. – A cottage. Hers – and her husband's.'

Fairhazel reached inside his jacket. 'We'll try another tack. It might be quicker.' The inevitable black notebook came out. There was a red elastic band round it. Fairhazel slid the band back over his wrist and opened the notebook. He took something out of it; it looked like a visiting card. 'Perhaps it was this lady,' he suggested, half rising and stretching out an arm.

It was a photograph, cut from a much larger one to fit the notebook. The edges were ragged, as if they had been cut with a pair of blunt scissors.

It was of the woman Michael had called Litvinova. The courier. It was greatly enlarged and very grainy. Most of her was blocked off by the crowd around her, but the locale was clearly the exit of St James's Park Tube station. She was about to step into a taxi. So they'd been tailing him. But since when?

'No, it wasn't.' He handed the photograph back.

'But you do know that particular woman, don't you, Mr. Coast?'

It was a try-on. A long-shot. He and Litvinova hadn't exchanged a word on the Tube, nor out in the street – except the one: 'Taxi.' She had said that as they stepped out on to the pavement, and uttered it to some point in the middle-air ahead of her.

'No. I've never seen her before.'

'She works at the Soviet Embassy.'

'I still don't know her.'

'You didn't share a taxi with her last Thursday morning?'

'Certainly not.'

'My man thinks you did.'

Thinks. That was the operative word: thinks. They didn't know.

'Then he thinks wrongly.' He tried a long-shot of his own. ' – Or perhaps your man managed to get a photograph of myself getting into the same taxi?'

Fairhazel made no reply, so clearly his operator had not. He laid the photograph back in his notebook and took out another.

'Or perhaps it was this lady?'

A passport photograph this time. Full face, unsmiling. A younger Roma Peterson. Christ, they really had been working quickly.

'No. It wasn't her either.'

'But you do know her?'

'Her name is Peterson.'

That photograph went back into Fairhazel's notebook. Without looking up, he said, 'When did you last see Mrs. Peterson?'

'June, I think. – In Paris.'

'You haven't seen her since?'

'No.'

'She says you have.'

'Then she's wrong.'

'How about her husband? – When did you see him last?'

'You know I couldn't possibly discuss that.'

'Mr. Mingay says you can. – I'll ask the question again, Mr. Coast ... '

'You know damned well. Look in the passport. You'll see why I couldn't have.'

'Couldn't have?'

His first slip. He daren't make another.

'My last visit to Paris was in June. If you don't believe me, look in the passport.'

'Not Paris, Mr. Coast. *I'm* talking about Hamburg. He says you met him in Hamburg.'

'Then he's not telling the truth for some reason. I haven't been to Hamburg in a year. Check the passport.'

'So both Peterson and his wife are lying? You're saying that?'

In a plan shot through with a million holes, that was the

only thing he had never really considered: that Peterson might go to the confessional-box.

'Yes, I am.'

'Why would they? Why would they, Mr. Coast?'

'I haven't the faintest idea.' He rose from his chair before his nerve broke altogether. ' – I'm going to get another – can I offer you one now?'

'No, sir. Thank you.'

He felt himself sinking into a haze of fatigue. They had suspected him since some time after Lomax had died. But all that was really important was that no one had followed him to London Airport on Friday evening. If they had not, he still had a few more days, days to contact Michael, days to plan his exit. They were going to have to get him out. And quickly.

An hour. A whole hour of weaving, twisting, dodging, staying just out of reach. The mythical lady-friend. The meeting in Paris, the meeting in Hamburg – Peterson must have squealed like a rabbit – and his wife with him.

' – It was over a strip-club on the Reeperbahn.'

'Look. I've told you. I did not meet Peterson in Hamburg.'

'He says you did.'

'Then he's lying.'

'Why?'

'God only knows. – I certainly don't.'

Fairhazel wasn't quite so sure of his ground here. You could smell it. Whoever had briefed him was equally unsure.

'But you did meet Mrs. Peterson here in London last week.'

'No. I did not.'

'Wednesday, to be precise.'

'Not any day. Sorry.'

'My man saw you both, Mr. Coast. You called at her hotel, and you both went out together for a spot of Chinese. Then the two of you went back to the hotel, and you reappeared on your own at about one-thirty and got back here at two o'clock. Your light was on till three o'clock. What did you do then? Go to bed?'

Christ, they must have practically been living in his pocket.

'All right,' he conceded. 'That bit of what she told you *is* true. Look ... ' back on with the chummy smile, ' ... I should tell you ... Mrs. Peterson and I were screwing-friends. It was brief, I hasten to add. And last Wednesday was pay-off night. I told her we were finished. She was angry. ... We had a row. ... A blinder. ... But it didn't concern Peterson ... security wasn't involved. I wouldn't have been so foolish.'

'So what you sat reading in your car weren't those telex numbers?'

'In my car?'

'Just off Brompton Road. With your courtesy-light on.'

He had thought it was a morass that Fairhazel was treading, a muddy gumbo of suspicion and guesswork held together by the dubious cement of Peterson's blatherings. But it wasn't. It was fifty-percent solid ground. He felt the chill sweat break at armpit, groin and palms.

'I've no idea what you're talking about.'

'She gave you a sheet of numbers that Mr. Peterson read out to her over the telephone. – He told her they were telex numbers.'

'No. She's lying.'

'Why should she lie? Why, Mr. Coast?'

'A grudge, perhaps. ... She's that sort of woman.'

Fairhazel didn't comment on that. And it became clear, even through the haze of fatigue and exhaustion, that however much the Petersons had confessed between them, whatever fingers had pointed at him, no one had seen him board the aircraft for Hamburg on Friday evening.

'But you do know something about an operation called Minaret?'

'A name. That's all. – Mr. Quilter mentioned it to me once. Twice, perhaps; I honestly don't remember. – But I was never privy to it. – I never knew who the man was – or the woman, for that matter.'

Fairhazel would be going soon. He had lost his momentum. Had just taken a covert glance at his watch.

He was tired. Immensely tired. And so much to do yet.

'What's that mark on your cheek, Mr. Coast?' Fairhazel touched his own cheekbone. 'How did you come by that?'

It was his right cheek. The patrolman on the autobahn wouldn't have seen it. Or would he?

'A door. – In the dark. – The cottage was unfamiliar.'

'The *Bundespolizei* say it was an Englishman.'

Another glassy smile.

'I'm not with you?'

'Minaret. – Whoever throttled him was an Englishman.'

'I'm sorry – you've lost me altogether.'

'His name was Tavistock. – Except that his passport number was a fake. – The passport people have checked it out. The number belonged to someone else.'

Fear was a tight collar and the metallic taste of copper.

'Look – can we get this straight?'

'Straight?'

'I don't know what you're talking about. Really.'

'Christ! – It's absolutely bloody ridiculous.' A laugh. It sounded like pouring gravel.

'We're pretty sure you flew out of London airport a few weeks back. – About the time Peterson says you met him in Hamburg. – As Tavistock. – We've checked back with the airline computers. – Very ubiquitous is Mr. Tavistock.'

'No. Sorry.' He'd told Michael how risky that was. Using that passport twice.

'But it's a coincidence, isn't it? – Tavistock goes to Germany twice, on one occasion when you drop completely out of sight. And you did drop out of sight, last Friday evening. – Like a hole in the ground, my chap said. – One minute you were there. The next you weren't.'

'I'm tired. – I'm sorry. – If this has to go on, I'd much rather we pursued it tomorrow.'

'I'm tired too, Mr. Coast. – But I'm close. – And I'm going to get closer. Perhaps tomorrow. Perhaps next week.'

'And I can get you for that. – Harrassment.'

'You'd have to prove it. Witnesses, Mr. Coast. – And just now, you haven't got a friend in the whole bloody world. – Take my word for it, Mr. Coast.'

Through the mist, Fairhazel was levering himself out of the armchair. Rising and hoisting the waistband of his trousers and buttoning his jacket.

'And now, if you don't mind, Mr. Coast, I'd like your finger and palm-prints.'

'Don't be ridiculous.'

'Here or down at the local nick, Mr. Coast. One way or the other. Suit yourself.'

Fairhazel had picked up the aluminium case from beside the chair he had been sitting in and was opening it on the coffee-table. He took out a pad of what looked like cartridge paper, an inking pad and a rubber roller.

It was all right. He'd wiped everything, been careful to touch nothing he hadn't remembered touching.

'I *could* play the outraged citizen.'

'Yes, Mr. Coast, you could indeed,' replied Fairhazel patiently. 'But you'd be wiser not to.'

Sweaty right hand, cold roller, down on the paper, fingers splayed.

Left hand.

Hitch the smile back while Fairhazel distributed his paraphernalia back in the case.

'And what happens now?'

Fairhazel clicked shut the catches of the case.

'It depends on the German police, Mr. Coast. They've got a walking-stick, you see. They think it was the murder weapon. And it's covered in what we call 'dabs'. They want to sort them out, that's all.'

Only with a tremendous effort did he restrain his bladder and stop his legs buckling beneath him. The stick. He hadn't wiped the stick! The room dipped and spun like a maelstrom. Oh, dear God!

Steady. Take a grip. They'll get you out. They promised.
'You won't be doing anything off the cuff, will you, Mr. Coast? – Like upping off to Moscow on the sly. – Because you won't make it.'

Now he was turning for the door and they were friends again.

'See you were a rower, sir.'

'Yes. – At Oxford.' – Another cackle. 'A long time ago now. – I doubt I could even shoulder an oar these days.'

'Anno domini,' said Fairhazel with surprising triteness. 'Happens to all of us.'

His broad back filled the doorway to the lobby.

' – And one last thing, sir.' Turning. Smiling. Hideously benign.

'Do you happen to have a street-map of Paris? – Like the one Mr. Peterson had?'

'I haven't the faintest idea what kind of street-map of Paris he had. – Or even if he had one.' And then he rolled for the biggest gamble of his life. He pointed to the bookcase, 'If I had, it would be in there. – Or take up the carpet if you like. – Take a look. – I've told you: you're on a hiding to nothing.'

But Fairhazel stayed where he was, his smile fixed because you've got rid of it already, you fly bastard.

'If I were you, Mr. Coast, I'd give your weekend lady-friend a bell on the telephone. – Be the best thing all round, would that.'

And then he was gone and it was still only quarter past two and felt like half past five.

Whitehall buzzed like a hive of bees. The people were normal, the buses were normal, the taxis were normal, and the sun still shone from the same direction and the pigeons still strutted with jerking necks. And it was like a nightmare.

He had jettisoned his last cassette of litho film down the side of the bus-seat that had brought him from Victoria. The Russian document-copying lens that the first Michael had given him had gone into one of the flats' communal dustbins in the early hours of the morning, the street-guide, and the code-pad he had never used, had gone down the lavatory, page by torn page, within minutes of Fairhazel's departure.

Up the steps. The show of his pass. The guard beamed genially at him.

He stood behind Goldring in the lift, could count the downy hairs at the side of her neck, smell her Old English Lavender perfume. He had started to ring Michael at six o'clock this morning and had gone on till eight. There had been no reply and that had never happened before. And he had quartered the passages of the flats and the forecourt and the pavement where the Fiesta had been parked, and couldn't find the girl's telephone number anywhere.

'What the hell's going on, Tony?'

Quilter was still hanging up his bowler hat and umbrella on his coat-stand. And he was very calm and very composed, even had the time to dump his briefcase on his desk and unbuckle it, and to take some papers out and lay them on his blotter. Then he smiled and said quietly:

'Do you know, Jocelyn, I was rather hoping *you* might tell *me* that.'

'He was waiting for me.'
'Yes, I'm sure he was.'
'It's ridiculous, of course.'
'Is it?' said Quilter, quirking one eyebrow. 'Really, Jocelyn, what an idiot you must think I am.' He reached down beside him and opened one of the drawers in his desk. He passed across a plain buff envelope that was unsealed, then a metal-framed reading-glass. He said nothing.

Tucked into the bottom corner of the envelope was a rectangle of plastic, thin and springy, the size of a postage-stamp.

'You'll need the glass,' Quilter said. 'Hold it up to the light.'

It was a photographic negative. A translucent background

covered with small black rectangles, and each of the rectangles was smothered with what looked like diminutive Arabic hieroglyphs. And although it was all too reduced to make anything of it, Coast counted the rectangles and guessed what it was at once.

'It's a frame of micro-fiche,' he said. 'What about it?'

'Oh, come, Jocelyn,' chided Quilter. 'It's the report you compiled about the RNAF back in May. – Minaret sent it back to the CIA as one of his love-tokens. All he didn't know was your name.'

'But most of the Section worked on that report.'

'Except Lomax,' corrected Quilter. 'And that report only ever came together in one piece in two offices here – yours – and Miss Goldring's. – And what you have in your hand, if you could see it better, is the final handwritten draft. – Which Miss Goldring is quite prepared to testify, in court, that she gave to you at the same as she gave you over the typescript.'

'So Goldring has a Russian boy-friend. One of the Embassy Ivans.'

Quilter smiled, still with infinite patience.

'Rubbish,' he said.

'When did you get this?'

'Too late,' replied Quilter. ' – Yesterday afternoon – at about four o'clock. It was like a hornet's nest, this office, yesterday afternoon, Jocelyn. The CIA from Grosvenor Square, the Special Branch, Mingay, David Tribe, a big-wheel from Six. – There was absolutely no end to it. – And we could not find you *anywhere*, Jocelyn. Not *anywhere*.' Quilter put his elbows on the arms of his chair and lightly tapped his fingertips together. ' – And Mingay will have to resign, you know. And perhaps I might have to, as well. – We made a total balls of it. *I* never did think it was Lomax – never thought it was you, mind, either – but I never thought it was poor old Lomax. – But Mingay – well, you know Mingay, don't you Jocelyn – all that Hanoverian oafishness and those ghastly socks. – Mingay thought it was poor Lomax and Lomax he made sure it was. Once you had spirited that miserable piece of paper into the poor man's briefcase. – Of course, I'm guessing, Jocelyn. – Clutching at straws as they say … '

'You gave me Mingay's job.'

'My job, Jocelyn. It was my job. – Mine and Tribe's. – Bait. – A fake. Something to tickle your palate, Jocelyn. – The one thing we could be sure about if ever it came back from Minaret.'

' – And it didn't, did it?'

'No. – Because you didn't have time.'

'Christ, you're a fool, Tony. – And you've got no proof!'

'Proof?' Quilter's hysteria suddenly broke. ' – I don't need it! – And if Tribe doesn't get you for one thing, then the German police will certainly get you for the other.'

'You're bloody mad. You're talking crap.'

'Get out, Jocelyn.' Quilter's voice trembled as he fought to recover himself. 'Don't even go into your office for your briefcase. – Wesley will parcel up your private things and send them on to you. – Your letter of suspension will come tomorrow. Recorded delivery.' His two fists lay bunched on his blotter.

'And now get out, Jocelyn. – At once. Go on. Please!'

Someone followed him up Streatham Hill, and as he turned into the flats he thought he saw another figure quicken its stride so that it passed behind him too quickly for him to see its face.

His cleaner had been, and gone again, and left a note reminding him to put his laundry out for tomorrow. He tried the Battersea number again, twice, three times, and there was still no answer.

And he began packing a small suitcase, very neatly, so little space, so much to put in it. And he would have to see the children. That was important. Especially Susan. And perhaps Frances. Couldn't tell them anything, of course. Something simple and slightly dramatic. Posted abroad. Somewhere exotic. A scarf, gloves; against the Moscow winter. Odd that his mind could focus on such trivia. A few whiskies helped to focus his concentration even more. That threat he had made to the girl last night. Stupid. It would have been better left unsaid.

The voice on the phone caught him by surprise because it had been answered after only the second ring.

'Michael? – Do you know, I honestly don't know. – I've only moved in here this morning. If you like I'll go downstairs and ask one of the other tenants. Would you like to hang on?'

And when he dialled the number again in case he had dialled it wrongly, the same cheery voice answered him.

And he knew that either something had gone seriously wrong. Or that they had ditched him ... that they had ditched him ...

'Frances?'

'Who's that?'

'Joss – Jocelyn.' Frances would understand. She always had. Too much sometimes. He held the bottle high so it didn't clink against the glass. Some whisky slopped on the sideboard, ran over the edge and down the front.

'You sound different.'

'No ... no ... not really.'

'Are you ill?'

'No ... no. Not ill.' A cigarette, unlit, clamped between his fingers. He couldn't remember how it had got there. ' ... How are the children?'

'Fine.'

' ... Don't ring off ... '

'You sound drunk.' Hard, accusing. She had never used to be.

'No. ... I'm not. ... Really, I'm not. Frances ... look ... Something's come up ... '

'I can't hear. You're mumbling.'

'Something's come up. ... Look ... can I drive across for a few minutes this afternoon?'

There was a sigh. A Frances sigh. One of her oh, God, what an almighty balls-up all this is, kind of sigh.

'Joss, I'm getting married on Saturday. Remember?'

No, he'd forgotten. And anyway it wasn't important any more. By Saturday he would be gone. It was only the intervening days that he had to live through. Next week it would all be different.

'A few minutes. ... I promise not to keep you. ... If you say go, I'll go.'

Then a Frances silence. He thought she had gone, prayed she hadn't.

'Oh, all right. – But well after lunch. About three. – And the place is like a tip but you'll have to put up with it.'

'Yes ... yes ... I really don't mind. ... And I won't keep you long.'

'Don't worry. You won't. – Goodbye, Joss.'

Then he tried Battersea again, and the voice at the other end was the same.

Eighteen

He had driven here like an automaton, with tunnel vision, the whisky bottle on the floor beside him in case he needed it.

He aimed himself across the grass and towards the gate. There was a FOR SALE flag strapped to the right-hand post, with a SOLD sticker pasted across it like a triumphant afterthought. It had rained here. The path was still wet and rain still dripped from the shrubbery in the sunshine.

When Frances opened the door to him, she looked, he thought, very pale, very tense. For the first time in years she had a cigarette in her hand.

The hall was littered with cardboard boxes and tea chests. He wended his way with a robot's precision between them. A lone tea-cup that he seemed to remember stood on top of a boxful of others all cocooned in old newspapers. A yellow tea-cup. Gold rimmed.

She was waiting for him in the dining-room amidst more cardboard boxes – of books and china – odds and ends – rubbish. Just standing there. Looking at him.

'Sorry, Fran,' he said, smiling vacuously at her and trying to bring her more into focus. ' – Bit pissed. – Sorry. – Really.'

She said nothing, for some reason found it difficult now even to meet his eye.

'I am, Fran,' he mumbled again. ' – Really fucking sorry.'

'What do you want, Joss?'

'Talk,' he heard himself say. 'I need to talk to somebody.' He shouldn't have come. It was always the same. She was hard, tough, tougher than he had ever been. Her stance was stiff, one arm hugged across her, its hand tightly clamped in the elbow of the hand that held her cigarette. He waited for the tirade. But it didn't come. And there was an aura about the place that felt like tension. Bright patches on the wallpaper, where pictures had hung. Lonely here now. Cold. Even in the sunshine.

'Can we ... sit down?'

' ... Yes. If you have to.'

He reached for the nearest chair. Heal's they had bought that from. Five of them and a carving-chair, and the oval table. – After the year in Bonn, when they had finally come back to settle in the house at Godalming. Strange. He felt strange. Unfamiliar. Bonn had been the last of the good days. Sunday afternoon, the trams clattering by down below on the street, yesterday's London newspapers on the coffee-table and young Simon having a nap along the passage with his thumb in his mouth and smelling of soap and baby-powder. The light pressure on the back of his armchair, Fran's hair falling over his face and her inverted face kissing him. I'll go for a shower. Put on a face. I'll call you.

' ... You came to talk.'

' ... When are you moving out. ... Soon, is it? ... '

' ... Tomorrow. ... The morning ... '

He lit a cigarette with numb fingers. Fumbling. She waited, offered no encouragement except to push an ashtray nearer. The last time he had seen her she had looked thirty-five. Today she looked a haggard fifty.

'Where are the children?'

'Out. ... What have you come to say, Joss, for Heaven's sake? ... I really don't have time ... '

He peered up at her. She was all over shaking. Staring down at him as if she was frightened to death of him.

'I'm getting out of the country, Frances.'

He expected something in reply that was pithy and biting. Why? Somebody's husband after you, is he?

But nothing came.

'It's a police thing,' he said. ' – And I've been suspended from duty. It's nonsense, of course. – There's been a leak — several leaks.'

'Leaks?'

' – Of information. Out of the Section. – The Section I work in. The stupid thing is that really all the indications point to Eric Lomax. I think I told you that.' Or had he? He couldn't remember. Not that it mattered any more. 'Everybody thought it was Lomax – I even found a page out of a restricted file in his briefcase. I mean, that *was* hard evidence, wasn't it?'

And now he was talking, all the things coming out in a gabble, not really what he had come here to say at all. It suddenly seemed important that she should understand, even the minutest details.

'*You* found it? – *You* did? – That piece of paper that all the trouble was about?'

He screwed up his eyes to see her better. She sounded like a bad actress in a bad play who had been rehearsing her lines all day and even now was terrified of fluffing them, her voice tremulous and pitched much too high.

' – or did you put it there, Joss?'

She would never know what a relief it was to hear her say that. It was as if he had been a flimsy dam holding back a monstrous weight of water, and suddenly a hairline crack had appeared. And from that crack had radiated another and another until the whole frail structure was a lattice of cracks and the seep of water became a roaring flood.

And he tried to explain to her how he had never thought it would come to anything. How he had thought that they would investigate old Eric and find out that it wasn't him – but that would take a few weeks – and those few weeks would give him time.

' ... Time for what?'

She had always been so sharp before. So perceptive; and he had to explain it to her patiently, the way he might have to Susan. – About this traitor in Moscow who had to be caught because of the damage he could do. Enormous damage. The K needed time to find him. And what had been so important, had been that a lot of stuff this treacherous bastard in Moscow was pushing out was Section stuff and in the end it could all be traced back to *his* desk. – That's how it was.

And he really was pissed and he really was fucking sorry, but he wanted to talk to somebody. Like the Catholics. That little box with the fretworked screen. He was terrified they were going to let him down. – The K. The KGB.

And still she didn't seem to know what he was talking about, and he screwed up his eyes at her and corrugated his forehead. Some change had occurred in Frances. She didn't like him any more. And she was lighting another cigarette from the stub of the other the way Lomax used to do.

Still scowling, he brought the two images of her into the one blurred shape.

'Oxford,' he said. 'They recruited me at Oxford. I think one of the dons put them on to me.'

'They?'

'The Soviets,' he said. 'They needed people.'

'I don't know what you're talking about.'

'Agents,' he explained. 'People in the right sort of places to find out things for them. Spies – you know.' He wondered if he ought to spell it out for her. S-P-I-E-S. 'The KGB.'

'Don't be ridiculous.'

And even when he was telling her the truth she didn't believe him and he thought how just like a bloody woman that was.

'That little man you saw me with that Sunday. The one you said looked like Uriah Heep – he was KGB. *You* remember. – Our last year – you thought I'd stood you up.'

She shook her head. 'No. No, I don't remember.'

'Surely you do.' It was important that she remembered, she was part of all this. A short man in a navy-blue suit, round shouldered. *So* high. Borisenko, his name was. Nikky Borisenko. ' – But I told you some other name at the time – I said he was one of Father's friends – ex FO.'

No. She was adamant. She didn't remember. She walked a

couple of paces to the window and became a silhouette, with her back to him.

So much to tell her, so little time. Random thoughts that fluttered about like gaudy butterflies that had to be caught at whatever the price.

The 'phone that rang late at night or in the early hours, the rings when there was no one at the other end. Sometimes they had frightened her, especially when he was out. Once she had 'phoned the police and made a formal complaint about them. They were Michael's telephone calls. There had been several Michaels. Michael was a code. A code-name. He was Anthony.

He had never whored, never done it for the money. He was a dedicated, committed Communist. Order was the thing. Say what you like about the Russians, they held order. It was the Russians who had finally put the boot in where the Fascists were concerned. Without the Russians, Western Europe would be a vast Fascist state by now. It wasn't the Russians the West ought to be worrying about. But all the Fascists hell-bent on creating disorder. Like a festering wound. Like cancer cells. Malignant.

It had been a career. His life. More important than his life. *That* important.

Then something she had said a long, long time ago surfaced, like a bubble of foul gas in a stinking pond, and he had a moment of blinding insight.

'How did you know I put it there? – How did you know, Fran? – No one's been – have they?'

She shook her head. Quick. Nervous. And he didn't believe her. And the house was very quiet.

There was no need for the kids to know. He had a couple of thousand on deposit in the bank. It could be shared between them. He would be gone before it all blew up. – They were working on it now – a passport, a passage out. Michael was. They wouldn't let him down.

'You sound doubtful,' she said. She had moved away from the window.

It wasn't just down to him, that awful business with

Lomax. – He wanted her to know that. – A lot of it was down to Tony bloody-Quilter. Quilter had gone along with it. And Mingay. Mingay had wanted it to be Lomax. Quilter had said exactly that this morning – or something dam' near enough like it. – So it wasn't all his fault, you see, Fran.

' ... So when are you going, Joss? ... Fixed a date?'

This was more the old Frances. The tough Frances with the out-thrust chin and the querulous tilt of the head. The Frances with the light of battle in her eyes.

' ... Soon. ... By the weekend. ... ' There was only a 'phone call to make.

'I lied to you, Joss. They came last night. And the kids were here and Donald was here. – And it wasn't nice, Joss. – I didn't believe them. I didn't believe them because I didn't want to believe them. They told me you'd killed somebody. – As well, I mean.'

And he had to screw up his eyes again to try and understand what she was saying.

' ... Had to Frances. ... He recruited me ... knew me.'

'I'm sorry,' she said, and sounded suddenly dreadfully tired. ' ... I can't carry on with this – and you must have what you need by now. ... I'm sorry.'

And he couldn't think why she was sorry. Until it slowly dawned on him that she wasn't talking to him at all.

* * *

Tribe and Fairhazel followed the two constables down the path. Between the two blue uniforms Coast walked with his head up and looked as if he hadn't had a drink in twenty years.

'Bloody nice woman,' said Fairhazel. 'She wasn't going to ring us, you know, sir. Took her all of an hour after he rung her. – She admitted that.'

One of the two constables had stopped to hold the gate open for Tribe, and Tribe in his turn held it open for Fairhazel.

'I reckon they dropped him,' proposed Fairhazel.

'Yes, very likely,' agreed Tribe. A few yards along the lane

Coast was being helped into a white car. 'One of the snags to being a traitor that is. – Never quite know who your friends are, do you, Charlie?'

And the lane receded and Coast said nothing and was going to say nothing.

They always looked after their own, and one day they would come for him and spirit him away.

Pfft! Like that.